THE LAZARUS PROTOCOL

MITCH HERRON 3

STEVE P. VINCENT

For Maree and Margaret Pratt.

1

"SHIT!" Mitch Herron cursed as more lights on the helicopter dashboard flashed red, joining the others already warning that his ride was doomed. "Can't you just cooperate?"

The helicopter responded to his plea by shaking violently and Herron fought to hold the stick steady. Just flying the chopper was difficult enough, but it was becoming harder with each passing second. As if to illustrate the point, another red light blinked on, adding a coolant leak to his many problems.

Escaping in the helicopter had seemed like such a good idea 10 minutes ago, now he was questioning the decision. He had taken off from a rooftop in Washington D.C., the same rooftop where he'd barely survived a fight with an assassin named Shade. After dealing with Shade – who'd killed the original occupants of the police chopper – Herron had stolen the aircraft. His current plight suggested he should have inspected it for damage first.

An alarm wailed. Herron scanned the instruments and gauges for the source, his brief stint of flight training in the military being tested to the limit. Though he knew how to get a helicopter up and down again, he'd never had to deal with this much trouble before.

After a second, the problem became clear – the helicopter was nearly out of fuel. One of Shade's shots must have blown a hole in the fuel tank.

It was a final flip of the bird from the assassin, stacked on top of another he'd delivered before his death. Herron had fought hard to eradicate the leaders of the Enclave – his corrupt former puppet masters – but only moments before his death Shade had taken great joy in telling Herron that his mission was incomplete. The Enclave's leadership hadn't been wiped out: its supreme leader – the Master – was still alive. If that was true, all Herron's work had been for nothing.

But he could worry about that later, if he managed to avoid crashing into the ground.

Knowing he was burning the very last of his fuel and that fighter jets had probably been scrambled to intercept him, Herron searched for a safe place to land amongst the forests and farmland below. He spotted a relatively flat field a few moments later. It was good enough. He couldn't push his luck more. There was too much wrong with the machine to coax any further performance out of it.

Running on fumes, Herron took the chopper down, the handling becoming even worse as he lost altitude. He gripped the stick tight. "Here goes nothing!"

Herron's eyes flickered between the instruments and the windshield as the chopper rumbled louder. Despite the flashing lights and blaring alarms, he tried to keep his cool. The last thing he needed in this situation was to panic or rush, even if the chopper was falling out of the sky more than landing. He picked a nice level part of the field and went for it.

Relief washed over him as the chopper touched down, but it lasted only a second. The loud squeal of twisting metal told him he'd landed too hard and one of the landing struts had buckled. Herron tried to compensate for the sudden imbalance, but he was far too slow to adjust the stick.

The chopper rolled onto its side and Herron grimaced as he was thrown around in the safety harness. The shriek of the rotors shearing off assaulted his ears and the smell of aircraft fuel filled his nostrils.

Then it was over. Herron coughed violently and shook his head to clear the fog. He reached out for the console, switched off the engine and cut the fuel. He didn't want to risk a fire. It would be the cherry on top of a cake made of shit.

Herron pressed the harness quick-release button and fell free, grunting as he landed hard on his side. Still coughing, he found his pistol and fired several shots into the already damaged windshield. Cracks spider-webbed through the glass and Herron kicked out, dislodging the glass in one badly damaged piece.

He struggled to his feet and carefully climbed out through the opening. He was sore from the fight with Shade and the crash, but he was in one piece. That's more than could be said for his ride. The helicopter was now a wreck of torn metal: the main rotor had sheared off, the tail rotor was buried in the dirt and the fuselage was badly damaged.

Time to move.

After stuffing the pistol into the waistband of his jeans, Herron picked a direction at random and started to walk. He needed to find a road, relieve someone of their wheels and stay ahead of the cops. It was slow going. He walked with a limp, pulling up short the few times he tried to run. He was going to have to do this the hard way – inch by inch across a field that stretched as far as the eye could see.

Herron had barely made it 500 yards before an explosion boomed behind him. He turned and looked back at the chopper. A fireball was streaking into the sky, wreathed by greasy brown smoke. Herron watched the chopper burn for a second, glad he'd made it out of the aircraft and wondering exactly what had caused it to blow. Then he resumed his walk across the field.

If the cops didn't know where to look before, they knew now.

* * *

"Damn it!" The speeding SUV kicked up a cloud of dust as it passed, its driver ignoring the thumb Herron had held up.

He stopped walking and coughed loudly to clear his lungs. His plan to commandeer a car hadn't worked – every passing driver had ignored his attempts to flag them down and he'd swallowed a lot of dust while trying. He was starting to get desperate. The cops would be closing in. He didn't want to use the pistol to force someone to stop, but he might not have a choice.

He made it another half-mile without seeing any more cars. For the first time since leaving the rooftop, he had time to think. He'd been so focused on escaping that he'd barely processed Shade's bombshell: that one of the Enclave's leaders may still be alive. If it was true – and he wasn't sure – he would have to get clear of the authorities before he could figure out what to do next.

A few minutes later, he heard the deep growl of a V8 engine approaching from behind him. Herron smiled. There was something magical about the sound and he decided he wanted that car. But when he turned his head and locked eyes on the vehicle, his smile disappeared immediately. It was a police cruiser – there'd be no chance of a ride in it on any terms he'd find favorable.

The roar of the engine increased as the cop car drew closer, but it was soon overwhelmed by the piercing wail of a siren. Herron sighed. It looked like they were going to do this the hard way. He waited as the cruiser pulled to a stop, its sirens blaring and light bar flashing like a disco.

He kept his hands relaxed by his side. On the surface, he looked calm and compliant, but he was coiled to strike. These cops might be pulling him over because they were bored, or they might know he was a dangerous man who'd crashed a chopper in their county. He was ready for both possibilities, keeping front-on to the cops so they didn't see the bulge of the pistol in the small of his back.

The lawmen killed the siren and climbed out of the car, leaving the engine idling. Maybe they thought he'd make a run for it and they'd need to chase him down.

Herron smiled. "Afternoon, officers."

Neither cop responded as they closed in, their eyes hidden by dark glasses. Both were in their late 20s and had plenty of tread left on their tires. Herron had hoped for a pair of lazy veterans, guys nearing a pension who'd rattle his cage a little and then move on. These two looked more ambitious, which made them more dangerous.

"Afternoon." One of the officers stopped a few steps closer to Herron than his partner. His nameplate read 'Riley'. "Decided to take a stroll?"

Herron shrugged. "Great day for it."

"Sure. Except we noticed you're all bloody and walking with a limp."

"A limping stranger with blood on them raises some questions around here." The other cop spoke around a mouthful of gum. The tag on his shirt read 'Davidson'. "Big ones."

Herron kept his eyes on Davidson. Of the two, he had his hand closest to his weapon. "I crashed my car a few miles back and my cell is flat. I was going to get help."

"Strange, we didn't see your car..." Riley's voice trailed off. "But it's your lucky day. We can take you into town."

Herron needed a ride, but a cop car wasn't what he had in mind. "Thanks, guys, but the thing is—"

The radio on Davidson's shoulder squawked. "*Dispatch to one-nine, receiving?*"

Davidson held down his talk button. "Receiving."

"*Say, Al, you guys spotted a crashed helicopter?*"

He shook his head and looked at Riley, who laughed. Davidson keyed the radio. "You drunk again, Mike?"

"*I'm serious, asshole. D.C. Metro Police lost one of their choppers and they're saying it came down somewhere near you guys.*"

Herron didn't like where this was going. He took a half-step back from Riley. "Sounds like you guys have a job to go to. I'll keep walking."

Riley frowned, as if something had just fallen into place in his mind. He drew his pistol and aimed it at Herron. "Don't move, pal."

Davidson tensed. "What is it?"

"Look at what he's wearing."

Herron looked down at his torn black combat fatigues. "They were on sale..."

Riley glanced at his partner, who also drew his weapon. "You're under arrest."

Herron didn't move. He could have drawn and downed both officers before either officer could fire, but he didn't want to kill these men. Instead he kept his features neutral as Davidson covered him. Meanwhile Riley moved in, holstered his weapon and started to pat him down. Herron paid close attention to where Riley's hands roamed, knowing that as soon as he found the pistol things were going to get messy. The cop started with his pockets, moved down his left leg and up the right, then felt around to his back. Herron winced as Riley reached the pistol... just as he heard sirens in the distance.

The situation changed from tense to insane in a second.

The instant Davidson glanced around at the convoy of police vehicles tearing toward them, Herron moved like lightning. He spun and used all his momentum to elbow Riley hard in the temple. As Riley dropped, Herron pulled his pistol from behind his back. He had the jump on Davidson now.

Herron advanced on Davidson with his weapon leveled. "Don't even think about being a hero."

"You're a dead man." Davidson sneered, but he kept still. "A half-dozen cops will be here in 20 seconds."

"Then there's no need for you to worry, because they'll take me down." Herron pointed to the ground. "Toss the pistol."

He waited until Davidson had thrown his gun in

the dirt, then ran to the police cruiser. He was glad the throaty V8 engine was still idling – the convoy of police vehicles tearing down the road was only seconds away. Herron climbed in the open door, shifted the cruiser into gear and floored it.

* * *

Herron clenched the wheel tight as the cruiser sped up to 80 MPH within a handful of seconds, keeping him just in front of the pursuit vehicles. Two stayed on his tail, while another had peeled off to assist Riley and Davidson. He'd stolen the police chopper to avoid exactly this situation, because the longer the authorities stuck on his tail, the more likely they'd catch him.

And Herron didn't intend to get caught.

He could let the pursuit chew up a lot of miles, but with each passing minute the chance of additional units joining the chase increased. He needed to end this soon. Luckily, he knew the cops' playbook and how to use it against them.

He eased off the gas and grinned as the pursuing cars closed in. "You sweet, predictable bastards."

As one of the cop cars took the lead, Herron watched it carefully in his mirrors. The driver was moving in to complete the standard PIT maneuver – Pursuit Intervention Technique – whereby he'd pull alongside Herron and steer into the rear of his car. Against most fugitives it would work like a charm, but against someone with Herron's experience it was a quick way to take yourself out of the chase.

Herron waited as the front of the cop car inched past his trunk, then slammed his foot on the brakes. The cruiser overshot, then Herron hit the gas. The V8 responded with a roar. He now had one cop car in front and one behind. Herron changed that quickly, pulling up alongside the vehicle ahead of him and executing his own version of the PIT. His car nudged the police vehicle, which veered off the road.

Herron righted his own course and smiled as the final cop car closed in behind him. He could see his pursuer's face in his rear-view mirror – the patrolman looked calm. It was time to change that. He eased off the gas, bleeding speed and letting the car on his tail get closer once again. He had to time his gamble perfectly. It'd hurt, but it'd work. When the chasing car was less than a yard from his rear, Herron clenched his teeth and hit the brakes.

He grunted when the patrol car slammed into his rear. He fought the steering and accelerated gently, trying to keep some power in the wheels. His car had taken a pounding but it kept moving, which was more than could be said for the other car. A glance in the mirror confirmed its airbags had deployed and it was stationary in the middle of the road, the driver likely stunned.

He'd done it. There was nothing except open road ahead of him...

...until he crested a shallow rise in the road and saw a roadblock a mile up ahead.

Herron narrowed his eyes as he tore towards the obstruction. There were two police cruisers parked across the road, their hoods pointed inward at each other. Four cops had taken cover behind the vehicles, their pistols drawn and aimed at Herron as he approached at high speed.

They were expecting him to stop and he was hoping they'd move.

It was a deadly game of chicken.

As his vehicle chewed up the distance to the roadblock, Herron had seconds to assess his options. Behind him were the cops he'd shaken off his tail and ahead were more of them blocking the road. There was no other place to go – he could charge ahead, turn around or give himself up. If he gave himself up he was as good as dead and if he turned around he'd still be in their net.

That left one option. The odds were abysmal, but his only choice was to punch through the roadblock and escape the dragnet that'd surrounded him.

Herron aimed his car at the narrow gap between the two police cruisers. If he hit the sweet spot, he might be able to get through. The airbags would deploy, but Herron hoped he could keep driving if the car wasn't too badly damaged. He made sure to keep the vehicle straight on and at full speed. Absolute precision and maximum force were the keys. He was a half mile out when one of the cops held up a hand...

Herron didn't stop.

A quarter mile out, the cops opened fire.

Herron ducked down as shots pinged into the cruiser's body and windshield like hail stones. He knew the engine block would protect his body, so he focused only on keeping the car on its driving line.

The world exploded.

Herron grunted and closed his eyes as his vehicle slammed into the barricade with incredible violence. He was hit painfully in the face and in the chest. There were so many sounds around him he couldn't process them. His grip on the wheel slackened for just a second, then he forced his eyes open. The airbag had deflated, he was through the roadblock and he could see open road ahead.

He floored it.

But the engine didn't respond. His car was losing speed, even with his foot on the gas. Smoke poured from under the hood and Herron pounded the wheel as the car slowed to a stop.

He kept his hands on the wheel as the cops swarmed around him. Though several pistols were trained on him and the cops were shouting at him, he waited calmly as the door was opened and he was dragged out of the car.

Keeping his feet, he let the officer twist his wrists behind his back and cuff him, but as soon as he was restrained, a cop kicked him in the back of his left knee and he stumbled. After another boot in the back, Herron was eating dirt.

Things had just got a whole lot more complicated.

2

"TWENTY-NINE... THIRTY..." Herron sucked in a breath as he completed his set of squats, then dropped to the floor and started to do push-ups. "One... Two... Three..."

He worked through the exercises with ease. He was used to more strenuous workouts but the police station holding cell didn't offer much space or many options to mix it up. Though the light exercise didn't do much to raise his heart rate or stress his muscles, it passed the time.

He was back in Washington D.C. a whole lot sooner than he'd planned. Though he'd been arrested in Virginia, the local cops had been happy to hand him over to the D.C. Metro Police to face their more serious charges – including multiple counts of murder for his attack on the Enclave leaders. He'd been transported to a police station and tossed into this cell.

A police officer walked past his cell – he caught Herron's gaze and sneered. Herron just laughed and kept working on his push-ups. Every cop in the station was on edge. They knew they had a dangerous man in their midst but didn't know his identity.

Eventually he climbed up off the floor, lay on the bed and stared at the ceiling for a long while, counting the cracks. He contemplated for the millionth time whether Shade had lied about the Enclave's Master being alive. Then, finally, he fell asleep.

His nightmares returned, as they did every time he slept, but they had been different since he'd captured and killed his handler. Herron had always thought the targets he eradicated for the Enclave had been vermin and although they'd populated his nightmares, he'd always felt they deserved what they'd got. But before dying, Herron's handler had taunted him with the knowledge that he'd killed innocents, people guilty of no more than getting in the way of the Enclave. Since then, his nightmares had tortured him even more.

The squeal of the cell door opening saved him from hours in the prison of his mind.

He opened his eyes and saw a pair of cops, including the officer who'd been patrolling the cells earlier, who was standing in the entrance to the cell and holding a shotgun. These guys weren't messing around. Herron climbed off the bed, held out his hands and waited as the two officers stepped inside, the one with the shotgun keeping his distance while his partner approached cautiously.

"Time for a heart-to-heart." The cop cuffed Herron then shoved him towards the door. "If you give us any trouble, we can arrange for you to fall down some stairs."

Herron was led out of the cell and through the station to an interrogation room, where his escorts gave him some coffee then left him alone. He drank the coffee while he waited. An hour later the door to the interrogation room opened again. Two men in suits entered and sat opposite Herron.

They watched him. He stared back.

Finally, one of the detectives broke the silence. "Nothing to say?"

Herron shrugged.

The detective sighed and started peppering him with questions. He asked for Herron's name, his background, his motive for shooting up an entire floor of a Washington D.C. office building, the identity of his fellow shooters...It was all pretty standard stuff, but Herron felt no reason to answer. He was waiting for an edge. Until then, silence was his ally.

Before long, the detective lost patience and pounded the table. "Who are you?"

Herron smiled. It was time to push their buttons a little. "You asked me that already."

"He speaks!" The detective exhaled loudly. "Given the job you did shooting up that office building, we figure you must be ex-military. If you are, we'll find out soon enough. We've got your prints...we've got your photo...there's no hiding from this. Refusing to cooperate just puts you in deeper shit."

Herron crossed his arms. Right now there'd be cops trying to identify him by scouring every government database and law enforcement system in the country. They'd also be checking with the Pentagon and the National Personnel Records Center in St Louis – the US repository for information about millions of discharged or deceased veterans.

They wouldn't find anything.

Though Herron had been born in Chicago and spent a decade in the special forces, the Enclave had erased every record of him. He was a ghost. After completing a mission, he'd always shed one persona and replaced it with another, until it became so automatic it was like breathing. Regardless of the heat on him right now, his true identity was safe.

Despite the detective's confidence that Herron's identity would soon be cracked, the interrogation returned to form: the detectives asking repetitive questions that Herron refused to answer. He had no intention of doing time, but he couldn't yet see a wrinkle he could exploit to get out of this situation. In the past, he'd have relied on the Enclave to spring him loose, but he was on his own now that he'd gone rogue and eradicated their leadership.

Or most of their leadership, if Shade was to be believed.

By now Herron was growing tired of the endless questions. Time to change the dynamics. He spoke the four magic words hated by cops everywhere. "I want a lawyer."

"You want a lawyer?" The detective sneered at him and glanced at his partner. "Didn't we offer him one of those a few hours ago?"

The other cop nodded. "Are you sure? If you talk to us now, we can help you. But once a lawyer walks through that door you're on your own."

The good cop had made his play.

Herron sat, face impassive. He wondered if there was some sort of script these guys followed and if the crooks ever fell for it. They had a slam dunk case against him, but they'd been trying to coax his identity and a confession out of him. A lawyer would complicate that. But Herron had made his request and they'd have to comply with it.

The good cop sighed after a minute or so. "Suit yourself, we'll get a lawyer in to talk to you, but you're making a big mistake."

* * *

Four hours later, after another workout and a meal in his cell, Herron was in a different interrogation room. It looked the same as the ones the detectives had questioned him in earlier, except this one didn't have a one-way mirror. That meant his lawyer was on the way. The cops had even removed his cuffs, so he sat back in his chair with his hands behind his back and his eyes closed.

After another five minutes Herron heard the door open. He opened his eyes. A woman was being escorted into the room by a uniformed police officer, who then left and closed the door behind him. Herron summed up the woman. She was young, nervous, clutching a manila folder tight in both hands, like she expected someone to snatch it from her.

After standing frozen in place for a second, she stepped closer to him and held out her hand. "I'm Renee Elder. I'm your court-appointed lawyer."

Herron smiled at the woman and shook her hand. "Who'd you piss off to get this job?"

Elder gave him a cautious smile. "I wanted to do some community legal work before I join a firm."

"Your family firm?" Her face flushed red. It was obvious she was a rich kid wanting to slum it a while before hitting easy street. "Good for you, kid."

She opened the manila folder and took a second to organize herself, removing paperclips from documents, stacking the paper into working piles, picking up a pencil. When she was finished, she looked at him expectantly. Herron wanted to see what she was made of, so he simply returned his hands behind his head and kept his eyes locked onto her.

Finally, she spoke. "What do I call you?"

"You can call me Bob."

She scribbled the name on her pad. "Is that your real name?"

"No."

She sighed and put the pencil down. "Listen, I've reviewed your case. You're in a lot of trouble. You're facing a list of murder, assault and firearms charges as long as my arm and a pile of minor charges thicker than most novels. You're lucky D.C. doesn't have the death penalty, but you need to start playing ball. What are you hoping to achieve, Bob?"

"I have no intention of spending my life in a small box, put it that way. I just have to figure out how to avoid it."

She laughed. "You're ambitious, I'll give you that. But there's no way you're avoiding time. You need to reconcile with that. The only thing up for grabs is how long you're in for."

Herron nodded. In truth, he only needed one thing from her. "Can you tell me when I'll be moved into the general prison system?"

"After your bail hearing. If that fails – and it will – they'll move you within a day or so. Forget that, though. We need to talk strategy. I'd suggest we wait until the medical situation with the survivor is clearer. Once we hear what he has to say we might be able to push for a plea bargain. You'll be facing a little less jail..."

Herron tuned out of the conversation. Before, he couldn't be sure that sadistic asshole Shade hadn't been screwing with him, but now he had independent verification that there was a survivor and that changed everything.

He locked eyes on Elder. "Who survived the shooting?"

She glanced down at her notes. "Robert Pritchard. He's being treated at George Washington University Hospital for minor wounds and shock."

Herron couldn't be certain the name was real or that the survivor was the Master, but he had to take the information seriously. He and his team had turned the office building into a kill zone, and he had no idea how anyone could have survived it, but he wanted to find out. He needed his freedom as soon as possible, because if this Pritchard only had minor injuries they wouldn't keep him in hospital for more than a day or so.

"I'm guilty."

She frowned. "What?"

"I'm guilty." Herron stood. "Don't contest bail. I want to go to a proper jail."

Slowly, she nodded and then got to her feet. "I think you're making the right decision. If you behave in jail and play ball with the authorities, we might get you out before you die."

Herron walked around the table. As they shook hands, he reached behind his back with his left hand and snagged a paperclip from her notes on the table. He kept his eyes on her the whole time and she didn't notice; the only risk was that she'd realize later it was missing and alert the authorities. It was a gamble, but he was a man used to those.

He closed his fist around the paperclip and let go of her hand. "How long will it take for them to move me?"

She shrugged. "I wouldn't be surprised if they had you on the bus tonight."

* * *

Herron smiled as the door on the bus closed with a hiss and the driver started the engine. The throaty diesel roared to life, probably the only part of the rust bucket that'd had seen any maintenance over the last decade. The prison district had likely purchased the bus for next to nothing and converted it into an inmate transport for cheap.

He didn't mind the condition of the vehicle. He didn't plan on riding for long.

Herron whistled a tune as the driver shifted into gear and hit the gas. The bus lurched forward and they were soon on the road. Even though Herron's ankles were cuffed to the floor and his wrists were secured to the rear of the seat in front of him, he couldn't be happier. Elder had been right. The transfer had happened quickly once he'd been denied bail. He was one step closer to freedom and dealing with Robert Pritchard – the Master.

He had a new mission. He had a purpose again.

Apart from the driver, Herron was the only person on the bus. He sat back in his seat and waited. Time was on his side. As he'd been led up the stairs onto the bus, he'd taken a peek at the driver's schedule. It had confirmed he was being transported to Chesapeake Detention Facility – a supermax prison in Maryland. Elder had told him Maryland had a contract with the Federal Government to house pre-trial detainees charged with crimes in the capital, so the transfer made sense.

As the bus ground through the miles, and suburban D.C. gave way to countryside, the sun sunk over the horizon and night settled in. Soon enough, the inside of the bus was dark, illuminated only by the ambient light that spilled in from cars passing in the other direction. Herron doubted their drivers had any idea of the dangerous cargo that was passing them as they headed home to their families.

He went to work.

He spat softly and caught the paperclip as it fell from his mouth, where he'd held it the entire time. He bent the metal into shape, keeping his eyes on the driver, and once he had the smaller end sticking out perfectly straight, he twisted the rest into a makeshift handle. Finally, he reached up and bit into the end of the straight part, hard enough to leave an impression in it.

He waited until a car passed and admired his handiwork in the briefest moment of pale light, then he started work on the handcuff lock. Like every pair of handcuffs the world over, its mechanism was held in place by three ratchets with teeth. Using the paperclip, Herron was able to push them out of the way. In less than a minute his wrists and ankles were free.

Once Elder had confirmed the Master was alive, Herron had shifted his focus to the prison transfer.

Movement was the most vulnerable part of any security operation, whether it was transporting prisoners or the President. Any static position could be locked down and secured, the target protected by so many eyeballs and guns that things became difficult, but a lone driver in a vehicle was way more vulnerable to external threats.

Or internal ones.

Keeping hold of one of his cuffs, Herron dropped the paperclip and stalked forward, moving as quiet as a whisper. Whatever sound he did make was easily smothered by the rumble of the diesel engine. The driver was looking straight ahead, his mirrors useless in the darkness, the radio playing generic easy-listening tunes. The man wasn't prepared for what was to come.

When he was a step away, Herron pressed the pointed tip of the handcuff arm hard into the driver's throat. "Keep driving, straight and steady. What weapons do you have?"

The driver tensed, but he complied instantly. "Pistol in the holster and shotgun in the foot well."

Herron pressed the handcuff into him a little harder. "Hand over the shotgun. Count aloud to five, then hand me the pistol, count to five again and pull the bus over."

Herron watched the driver carefully as he kept one hand on the wheel and used the other to reach down for the shotgun. He took possession of the weapon, pumped the slide and aimed it at the driver. Now he had a whole lot more firepower than a pair of handcuffs. The driver counted to five, removed his pistol from its holster and then held it out for Herron, who took it and waited while the driver counted down again and pulled over.

"Good. Keep co-operating and you'll get out of this alive." Herron took a step back. "Now stand up, empty your pockets, and take off your pants and shirt."

The driver put the bus into park and killed the engine. After a glance at Herron, he stood and emptied the wallet and cell phone from his pocket. Then he removed his shirt, shoes and pants. Once the guard was standing in nothing but his underwear, Herron gestured him to sit down again and tossed him the handcuffs. This time, the man didn't need instructions; the message was clear. He cuffed his wrist to the wheel.

"You're home free." Herron shifted his aim. "This is going to be loud."

Herron fired the shotgun at the driver's radio. The boom of the long gun was devastating inside the enclosed space, and the result was similarly spectacular – the radio exploded in a mess of plastic. As the sound of the shot faded, Herron reached over and took the driver's keys from the ignition. The man was now stuck in the middle of nowhere and unable to contact anyone. He'd eventually be found, but by then Herron would be long gone.

Taking a step back from the driver, Herron rested the shotgun on the same seat where he'd stashed the pistol, then changed into the driver's pants and shirt.

They were a little big, but they'd do for now. He kept his own shoes. Now he looked little like the prisoner who'd climbed onto the bus, which might be the difference between success and failure. Satisfied, Herron took possession of the pistol and left the shotgun where it was.

The last things he did before leaving the bus was rifle through the driver's wallet for some cash – about eighty bucks or so – and then throw the wallet and the cell phone to the other end of the bus. Then he took one more look around, stepped off the bus, and took a deep breath of cool night air.

It tasted like freedom.

3

"FANTASTIC." Herron sighed as he turned up the car's radio, after the music had been interrupted by a newsflash. He didn't have to be Nostradamus to guess what the bulletin would be about. He'd been waiting for it since he'd escaped from the bus an hour ago.

The newsreader sounded earnest as he fired the starter's gun on a nationwide manhunt. *"Authorities are searching for a man who has escaped from custody. While police haven't released his name, they have revealed that the fugitive is charged with multiple counts of murder. The man is in his mid-thirties, has brown hair, and is armed—"*

Herron killed the radio and sighed again. He'd hoped for more time.

After escaping from the bus, he'd sprinted for a mile before reaching a grocery store. There, he'd stolen a car from the parking lot and hit the road, heading back to D.C. and hoping he could terminate the Master and complete his work before the cops realized he'd escaped.

So much for that.

Things were getting hot. Common sense and his training dictated that Herron go to ground until the attention from the cops had eased off a little. A man with his skills could remain invisible, but if he stayed out in public with all eyes searching for him there was a high chance he'd have further confrontations with the authorities.

But Herron didn't plan to hide, not until the Master was dead. He just had to move faster than law enforcement could catch up.

He turned into the parking lot of George Washington University Hospital and did a long, slow lap. As he drove, Herron searched for cops or anything else out of the ordinary. It all seemed fine. The parking lot was sparsely occupied and there were very few people around. It was past visiting hours, so the only cars he was competing with for space belonged to patients and the overnight staff.

Satisfied he was good to proceed, Herron parked as close to the entrance as possible and got out of the car. He was still dressed in the prison bus driver's black pants and white shirt, but it was as good a disguise as any. He crossed the parking lot and entered the hospital through the emergency entrance.

The emergency room waiting area wasn't overly busy, which wasn't surprising given it was 11:00 PM on a weeknight. Herron had been counting on that.

Before he was in sight of any hospital staff, he placed his left forearm across his chest and gripped it with his right hand, as if he'd injured it. Then he made his way to the reception desk.

The nurse behind the desk looked up from her computer. "Do you need help?"

"I think my arm might be broken. I was hoping a doctor could take a look at it."

"We can manage that. I'll just need a few details about you first."

Herron nodded and answered the woman's questions. He gave her an identity he'd shed a while ago – James Baker – a fake name that would show up on her screen as having full medical insurance. He hoped that would reduce the number of other questions he'd need to answer.

Money talked.

"Thanks for your patience, Mr Baker." The nurse smiled at him, satisfied with his credentials. "My colleague Tonia will take you through to a cubicle and get you seen to."

Herron followed Tonia through a security door and into the emergency room proper. The large space was dominated by a nurses' station, which sat in the middle and was ringed by a few dozen small emergency cubicles. Herron didn't speak to the nurse as she led him to one of the alcoves, pulled back the curtain and gestured for him to enter.

When he was inside and seated, she spoke. "Another nurse will be around to check your vitals, and a doctor will be in shortly."

Herron nodded. A second later, the nurse closed the curtain and left him alone. He waited for a couple of minutes, and then stood and slipped out of the cubicle. In his head, a clock started, counting down the time until he'd be exposed.

He walked through the hospital like he owned it. There were only a few other patients and staff moving around and none of them paid him any attention. He exited emergency and headed for a staff locker room.

He looked left and right. The coast was clear, so he pushed the door open and entered. The change room was just as empty as the rest of the hospital. Herron forced open a locker at random and smiled when he saw the clothes inside. He'd look like a doctor in no time. He changed quickly, transferred the pistol to his new clothing and threw his old clothes in a waste bin.

He stepped outside and headed down the corridor in the direction of the wards. When he arrived, he smiled at the woman on duty at the nurses' station and rounded the desk. He looked at the whiteboard, searching for Robert Pritchard's room number.

He was in Room 7...and seconds away from death.

Herron walked deeper into the ward. The numbers on the doors of the large suites he passed increased until he reached Room 7.

He looked around to make sure he was alone, drew his pistol and pushed the door open.

His mouth fell open. The hospital room was empty.

* * *

Herron shook off his moment of surprise and moved inside the hospital room. There was an armchair, some hospital equipment, a bed and little else. The bed had been slept in, but the patient who'd occupied it was gone. Suddenly, Herron's plan to terminate the Master was in disarray. He had to adjust.

He returned to the corridor, looked left and right, then approached the nurse at the nurses' station. "Where has the patient in Room 7 gone?"

The woman frowned. "He discharged himself only a few moments before you got here, doctor. We loaned him a wheelchair and he's on his way to the parking lot."

Herron kept his composure, but his mind was shouting curses. "I need to see him before he goes. Which way would they have gone?"

"To the elevators." The nurse pointed down the hall, then her face wrinkled with confusion. "Excuse me, doctor...I'm sorry, I just haven't seen you around before, and I—"

Herron turned and broke into a run. He was certain the Master was still in the hospital, but now, with his ruse exposed, time was of the essence. As if to illustrate the point, an alarm started to wail throughout the hospital. Security and the police would soon be on him.

He had to come up with a new plan. Fast.

Herron barely slowed as he raced around the corner and spotted an older, male nurse pushing a guy in a wheelchair. That had to be him: the Master. Both the nurse and the Master were oblivious to his presence, the nurse reaching out to press the elevator call button.

Herron drew his pistol and leveled it at the pair. "Hold it right there!"

The nurse turned and his eyes widened. "Don't shoot!"

Herron slowed to a walk and inched closer. The man in the wheelchair craned his head around and they locked eyes. Herron snarled. He was face to face with the Master for the first time. The minor setback had been corrected. He shifted his aim from the nurse to the Master, ready to eradicate this stain on the tapestry of humanity...

Then he sensed movement in his peripheral vision.

Herron grunted as someone tackled him from behind, a split-second before he had the chance to fire. As the heavy weight of a hospital security guard took him to the floor, Herron lashed out with his elbows and the pistol, trying to club the man off him. He landed a few blows, but then a second guard was on him, laying into him with a baton.

Herron rolled up into a ball, protecting his head from the assault. The guard who'd tackled him climbed to his feet and kicked the pistol away, then joined his colleague in whaling on Herron with his baton. Though the blows hurt, they were like getting kissed by a lover when compared with the pain of failure, knowing that with each second that passed the Master was slipping further from his grasp.

After a moment, the guards stopped laying into him. One of them slapped his baton against his palm. "Had enough, pal?"

Herron nodded, uncurled himself and glanced toward the elevator. The nurse had taken a step back and was holding his palms out in front of him, clearly terrified. His patient had abandoned his wheelchair and the door to the emergency stairs beside the elevator was slowly swinging closed.

Yet again, the Master had slipped from Herron's grasp. He needed to get after him, but before he could do that he had to deal with the security guards.

Herron looked at one of the guards. "Can I sit against the wall until the cops arrive?"

The guard nodded. "Fine. But make one wrong move and we start hitting you again."

Herron pushed himself across the floor to the wall. Both guards kept watching him, even as one of them stepped forward with the baton at the ready and the other reached down to secure the pistol. When Herron reached the wall, he used it to push himself to his feet. The guards stepped forward to stop him, one shouting at him to sit back down, but it was too late. Their mistake would doom them.

Herron stepped closer to them and they backed

away. Their batons were held at the ready and they probably had the upper hand, but their retreat told Herron they didn't think so. Here he was again, having to hurt innocent people who got caught in the crossfire – exactly the reason he rebelled against the Enclave in the first place. Once the Master was dealt with, he was going to stop.

Herron charged at the first guard, who swung the baton at him in a wide arc. Herron caught his wrist, twisted it down and away, breaking it in a flash. The guard shrieked in pain, dropping the baton so he could grip his fractured arm. Herron followed the strike with a sharp kick to the guard's knee. It buckled and he fell – he was out of the fight and there was no need to inflict any more punishment on him.

"Don't hurt me!" The second guard tossed the pistol onto the ground and backed away. "Please, don't hurt me!"

"Be smart." Herron kept his eyes on the guard as he leaned down to pick up the pistol. The man didn't move or try to impede him, so Herron didn't waste any more time.

Breaking into a run, he charged past the male nurse who'd been pushing the wheelchair and headed for the stairs. The alarm still blared and there was an electricity in the air, the hospital awake and active when minutes ago it had been sleeping and still. Patients were peeking out of their rooms and there were more staff members around than normal.

It wasn't a welcome development, but Herron

ignored them all as he charged through the door to the stairwell.

He took the stairs down two at a time. Pritchard was injured and only had a small lead on Herron, which meant there was a chance to catch him if he worked hard enough. There was no time for caution: things were getting hot at the hospital, but now was still the best time to get the Master. Herron had done everything right except finish his target, now he was at risk of failing altogether.

He could hear the *clomp-clomp-clomp* sound of someone else rushing down the stairs below him. When he was three levels from the bottom, there came the sound of a door slamming. Pritchard must have exited on the ground level. When he reached the bottom, Herron stashed his pistol in the waistband of his pants, put his hands on the door handle and opened it.

After a deep breath, he stepped out of the stairwell and prepared to hunt his prey.

Herron exited the stairwell and walked through the hospital towards the emergency reception area. There were plenty of security staff around, which was amazing given how deserted the hospital had been a little earlier, but Herron was dressed as a doctor and the security men didn't give him a second glance.

Still, he expected more heat on him at any moment, so he kept moving.

He looked around briefly, but he couldn't immediately see Pritchard. The Master had two options – try to double back and lose Herron inside the hospital, or head for the emergency room exit and try to outrun him. Herron made his own choice and headed in the direction of emergency. Soon he spotted a man in a hospital gown walking down the hallway in the same direction.

It seemed Pritchard had made his choice.

Herron followed his prey out of the hospital and into the parking lot. Two police cruisers were just pulling in, and Herron slowed down as they passed. News of the disturbance had clearly reached beyond the hospital. There'd be more cops on the way.

Herron returned his attention to where Pritchard was walking away.

The Master had gone.

Herron cursed, drew his pistol and was about to search the aisles between the parked cars when shots started to pound into the sedan beside him. There was no sound of gunfire, only that of the bullets' impact, which meant a silenced weapon. That ruled out the cops and made the Master the likely shooter. Several more rounds slammed into the car, but Herron was already moving. He crawled in between the vehicles, keeping his own pistol at the ready as he tried to locate Pritchard.

Herron flattened onto his stomach and looked under the rows of cars, smiling when he saw a pair of feet and the flowing bottom of a hospital gown. He rolled onto his side, aimed and fired at the Master's feet. The shots would alert the cops and security guards, but Herron didn't care. All that mattered was finishing the job. His smile widened when Pritchard cried out and dropped to the ground.

Jumping to his feet, Herron ran to where the Master lay. He kept his pistol aimed at Pritchard as he rounded the car and kicked his fallen foe's weapon away. It skidded under a car and out of reach. Herron had taken the last vestige of the Enclave to the ground and now, in a world of pain as he writhed on the concrete, the Master was completely defenseless.

"Bad luck." Herron kept the pistol aimed at Pritchard's head. "The Enclave dies with you."

"You know nothing." Pritchard scoffed. "What is dead can rise again. You should scurry under a rock, where you might just survi—"

Herron squeezed the trigger, putting a round between Pritchard's eyes. "155."

He exhaled, savoring the last and most important kill of his career. It was over. He knew he needed to go, but he waited anyway. He stared down at Pritchard's lifeless body, enjoying the sight of blood that was pooling on the concrete near his head. A split-second later, he frowned. Something was wrong...

Apart from the wounds Herron had given him – most obviously the bullet wound to the head – Pritchard was uninjured. The situation didn't match the story of a man in hospital being treated for injuries. So what happened to those injuries? Why had he been in hospital at all?

Only one explanation made sense.

The man oozing blood onto the ground wasn't the Master.

Herron closed his eyes and thought back to when he'd caught up with the man he'd thought was the Master and the nurse pushing the wheelchair. Small signs – the nurse wincing when he'd put his hands up, being less afraid than he should have been – told the whole story.

He'd fallen for the simplest of ruses. Pritchard had outwitted him. After checking himself out, Pritchard had swapped clothing with another Enclave operative and started pushing that man through the hospital. When Herron had intercepted them and chased after the patient, Pritchard had simply stood back with his hands up.

He'd killed an Enclave operative, not the Master.

Pritchard had escaped Herron's grasp and probably walked right out of the hospital.

"Fuck!" Herron opened his eyes.

The taste of victory was replaced by failure. He thought about going back into the hospital, but the Master would be long gone. Herron had lost contact with him over five minutes ago. He needed to get away from the hospital and plot his next move. If there was a next move. He turned and started to walk away from the hospital and the dead body...

"Freeze!"

He'd only made it a few steps when he heard the

shout and turned to see two police officers rushing in his direction. When they saw Herron's pistol and the dead body, they drew their own guns. Herron turned and ran, knowing that from this range the cops had an even chance of hitting or missing. The cops fired, but no bullets penetrated his body as he increased the distance from the cops.

Herron ran to the end of the lot, looking for an opportunity to escape. The cops had given up shooting and started to chase him, while even more police sirens were sounding in the distance. The heat on him was increasing with every passing second. He'd never been this exposed before, a man used to living in the shadows flushed out into the light. It was getting to the point where he could barely show his face in public.

When a driver in a nearby sedan pulled out of his parking space and drove in his direction, Herron was momentarily blinded by the car's headlights. Herron stopped running, shielding his eyes from the light with one hand while aiming his pistol at the car with the other. The driver was smart. He slowed the car to a stop and climbed out. Herron gestured for him to beat it and tracked him with the pistol as he ran away, then headed for the sedan.

Herron climbed into the car and put his foot to the floor.

4

HERRON CLENCHED his teeth as machine gun rounds tore chunks from the broad tree he was using for cover. The trunk protected his body but did nothing to silence the cacophony of gunfire that roared through the valley. Only escaping or eradicating his pursuers would achieve that and the odds weren't great.

There was a break in the gunfire, and Herron chanced a quick glance from cover.

It wasn't good.

A dozen infantry were advancing on him. He was alone, almost out of ammo and totally out of options. That didn't mean he'd make it easy on them. He aimed his rifle at an enemy soldier who'd drifted into his sightline and fired. The rifle kicked into his shoulder, the soldier dropped and Herron ducked behind the tree just in time as return fire barked out at him.

When the hail of bullets slackened, he ran further up the hill and sheltered behind another tree an instant before more shots tore into it. He was playing for time, but time was running out. There were only two rounds left in his rifle and he had no spare ammo. He looked down his scope, fired, worked the bolt action and fired again. Two targets fell, but the rest of the infantry kept advancing, taking advantage of their numbers.

Out of ammo now, he tossed the rifle on the ground and darted to the next tree. His luck ran out. Halfway to the next oak he grunted in pain as his left leg gave out from under him...

Herron woke with a start, sighed and rubbed his face. A glance at the alarm clock beside the bed showed he'd been asleep for barely three hours and already his dreams were taunting him. After escaping from the hospital, sheer exhaustion had forced him to go to ground. He'd swapped cars and used the bus driver's cash to buy supplies, clothes and a cheap motel room in the most out-of-the-way place he could find.

After crashing into bed, he'd fallen asleep quickly and a dream he hadn't had in a long time had returned with a vengeance. He'd been in the special forces when intel had come in suggesting a rogue North Korean general was preparing to launch an artillery attack on Seoul. Herron and his team had infiltrated, assassinated the general and then been ambushed on the way out. Herron had been the only survivor.

The timing of the dream was fitting, because the escape from North Korea was the only other time Herron had had so much heat on him. For the past few days – from the minute he'd left the rooftop in the helicopter to the time he'd climbed into the motel bed – the cops had only been a moment behind him. Law enforcement across the country were looking for him, his description was all over the news and his luck had almost run out.

All of that would be acceptable if he'd succeeded...

Herron put his hands behind his head and stared up at the ceiling. The room was illuminated by the pale-yellow glow of the alarm clock and what light from a streetlamp could peek in through a gap in the blinds. He wasn't a man used to indecision – he was given a target, he eliminated the target, then he waited for another one. But this time was different. Now he was a freelancer, he faced a choice: go to ground or keep on after the Master.

He didn't have to continue with this fight, but he wasn't sure he could live with himself if he didn't. The Master led an organization of elite killers, contractors like Herron who completed jobs on the understanding that their work was conducted on behalf of the United States Government and that those who died were human vermin. Herron had thought he was taking out terrorists, drug runners and other scum.

The resistance that'd formed against the Enclave had shown him otherwise.

So the decision was simple. He and the resistance had destroyed most of the Enclave, but it had to be eradicated down to the root.

The Master – Robert Pritchard, if that was his real name – had to die.

Herron didn't delay – he'd had enough sleep to power him for another day. He climbed out of bed, walked to the coffee table and opened the plastic bag of supplies he'd purchased from a gas station convenience store – food, water and the means to disguise himself. He took the scissors, shaving foam, razor and make-up from the bag, carried the items to the bathroom, and left them on the basin while he showered.

As the water pummeled him, he formed a plan. He'd fallen for a classic bait-and-switch at the hospital, giving the Master time to skulk back into hiding. Herron had to find him again. Unfortunately, he was not a woodsman tracking a dumb animal in a contained environment. He was looking for a hyper-intelligent man with billions of possible hiding places.

Luckily, he had an idea.

Herron turned off the taps, toweled himself off and returned to the basin. The cheap motel room didn't have a bathroom exhaust fan, so he used the towel to wipe the condensation from the mirror. He already looked a little different than usual, with a few days of stubble, several cuts and bruises. By the time he left the motel, he wanted to look like a completely new man.

Herron took the scissors to his already short hair. He cut as close to the scalp as he could, rough and fast, paying no attention to styling. When that was done, he filled the sink with hot water and applied the shaving foam to what hair remained on top of his head. He went slower with the razor, moving in slow and deliberate strokes, only pausing occasionally to rinse the blade.

When he'd shaved all the hair from his head, Herron considered his new look in the mirror. It was strange, but he did look totally different. After deciding to leave the stubble on his face, he drained the sink and started work with the makeup. He applied a layer of foundation, paying particular attention to covering up his scrapes and bruises.

When he was done, he ran his hand over his bald scalp and smiled. "A whole new man."

He didn't bother to clean the bathroom. He simply gathered up his possessions, turned the light off and left. He picked up the food and water from the coffee table, and after a quick breakfast of bread and honey, washed down with some water, he was good to go. He put everything he'd bought from the gas station into the plastic bag, tied it off and threw it in the trash.

Once dressed, he pocketed the car keys and left the motel room. He kept his eyes peeled as he moved towards his car – a stolen Toyota. He was used to camouflaging himself in the dark shadows of a city, revealing himself with precise and explosive violence only when needed, then hiding again. But with the entire country on alert, he had to be careful.

He unlocked the car, climbed inside and started it. He was going to take care of the Master, but he had to take care of someone else first.

* * *

Herron drove the Toyota to Frederick, Maryland. It was early in the morning and there'd been little traffic to slow him down, so the trip took only about an hour. He arrived in town just as the sun was starting to peek over the horizon and cars were starting to fill the roads; if all went to plan, he'd be gone before the sun was at its highest point in the sky.

He parked in the lot of a McDonalds restaurant and killed the engine. He squeezed the wheel tight and closed his eyes, hoping his guess was correct. The last time he'd been here, he had made one of the hardest calls of his life – agreeing to leave Erica Kearns behind as he drove off to fight the Enclave. He'd wanted to keep her close, but she'd insisted on staying behind.

It was the only time a personal conflict had threatened to impact on his mission.

If Herron died, nobody would know about it. The Enclave had scoured every trace of him from the world. His parents and siblings had never been much of a family and now they thought he was dead, he didn't have any friends, and there was no record of him anywhere. He was a dead man who walked the Earth and extinguished the lives of others. When his time came, he'd be a completely unidentifiable corpse – a John Doe quickly forgotten.

That didn't mean there was nothing that he cared about.

Before plunging into the most dangerous hunt of his life, Herron wanted to take care of Kearns, the one thing that mattered to him apart from his mission. He owed her. She'd brought him back from the dead, cured him of the deadly Omega Strain virus and then risked herself further to help him escape the police and get to safety.

He'd promised to return to her once the Enclave was dealt with, but if killing the Master cost his own life he wanted to make sure she was looked after.

He opened his eyes, climbed out of the car and crossed the parking lot. The McDonalds had only a couple of diners in for breakfast, people making the healthy choice to start their day. Herron entered and ordered, and when his food was ready, he walked to the booth furthest from the door and sat with his back to the wall. It was the best seat in the house, which let him see everyone who was coming and going.

As Herron ate, he kept his eyes on the door and the parking lot. Customers came and went, but not the one he was waiting for. He hoped she was still checking the restaurant – the place where he'd left her – every day. If she didn't show up, he'd have to search the other likely places: the grocery store, the post office, the restaurants and the cafes. But if she was smart she'd return here to the McDonalds.

Herron finished his meal and let an hour pass with no sign of her. It'd been a long shot, but it was the best one he had. He decided to wait another five minutes, aware of how risky it was to stick around. A cop could enter, a citizen could recognize him despite the disguise, or a staff member could wonder why the bald stranger was sitting around for so long after eating.

The time passed and Herron returned to his car, trying to decide where to look for Kearns next. He doubted she was working and he didn't know where she was living, so the only way to find her would be to catch a break as she went about her day. The grocery store seemed the best bet. He started the car, shifted it into gear and reversed out of the parking space...

...then he saw Kearns in his mirrors, right behind him.

He slammed on the brakes, a lump in his throat. She looked well. They'd been through a lot together, yet so much more than that had changed since he'd last seen her. Though it'd been less than a month, it felt like a lifetime. He watched her as she passed his car and headed into the McDonalds. She hadn't seen him and looked completely at ease as she ordered and waited for her food.

Herron was about to park the car again when another vehicle turned into the lot – a Frederick Police Department cruiser. The cops inside were driving at a normal speed and showing no signs of recognizing him, but their presence raised the stakes immediately. He'd wanted to go inside, meet with Kearns and explain the situation, but if he parked again and climbed out, the cops might recognize him.

"Fuck it." Herron cursed as he finished backing out and pulled slowly away.

He drove down the street for a few hundred yards, giving the cops enough time to get out of their car and inside the restaurant. Kearns wouldn't be going anywhere for a few minutes, so he had the time to play it safe. After a minute, he turned around and headed back, making for the drive-through.

The young woman staffing the window smiled at him. "Good morning, sir. What can I get for you today?"

"A large Coke." Herron smiled back at her and then glanced at his rear-view mirror. There was no one behind him in the line. "Can you also hand me a pen and some napkins?"

"Sure." She passed them out to him. "I'll just pour the Coke for you. Wait here please."

Herron rested the napkin on the dashboard and carefully wrote out a detailed set of instructions on the napkins, making sure each letter was perfect. He couldn't afford a mistake or for his writing to be illegible. The staff member finished pouring his Coke and returned to the serving window before he'd finished, but waited patiently until he was done. In all, it took three napkins to write his message.

"Sorry." Herron looked up at her and dug into his

pocket. He pulled out a twenty-dollar bill and handed it to her along with the napkins. "You can keep the change."

Her eyes widened as she took the money and the napkins. The tip was more than she'd make in a few hours. "Thanks."

Herron took the cup from her. "I need you to hand those napkins to a woman who's inside the restaurant. She's in her mid-thirties and wearing a denim skirt. It's very important."

"Okay." She nodded and looked down at the napkins. The words he'd scribbled on it wouldn't mean anything to her. She turned and walked away from the window.

Herron put the Coke in the cup holder and drove back around to the front of the restaurant. He didn't park, just sat with the engine idling and looked through the restaurant window. The drive-through attendant was already at Kearns' table. He watched as she handed Kearns the napkins, turned and returned to her post at the drive-through window – job done and tip earned.

Kearns read what was on the napkins – the location of one of Herron's stashes, along with detailed instructions on how to access it. The cache contained weapons and a million dollars, enough money to last her a long time if she used it wisely. At the bottom of the last napkin, he'd also written a farewell message. When the realization hit her, she looked up, but by then Herron was already on the road.

* * *

Herron revved the motorbike, accelerating enough to zip through the intersection before the traffic lights flickered from yellow to red. He relished the power of the bike beneath him – he'd stolen it from a backwater town somewhere between Frederick and Washington D.C – and while he was careful to stay below the speed limit as a precaution, that didn't mean he couldn't enjoy the ride.

He hadn't expected to return to the dragon's den so soon. With agencies all across the country after him, most people would consider heading back to the capital a crazy move – a suicide mission. But Herron knew he had no choice. He needed to get back on the trail of the Master and he had only one sure-fire way to do it: Michael Reeves. Reeves worked for the NSA, had helped Herron find his handler, and was a reliable resource for jobs like this.

When the most secretive people on the planet retreated into the shadows, they were almost impossible to find. The only answer was to deploy the world's largest spotlight – the NSA. Reeves had access to systems and data powerful enough to expose anyone. He would certainly be able to hack the security feed from the hospital and get a perfect picture of the Master.

Herron pulled up a half-block away from Reeves' apartment building and looked up and down the street. The lights were on in Reeves' window and the streets were deserted except for the occasional passing car. It was safe to proceed. He killed the engine, kicked down the bike stand and climbed off. With his crash helmet still on his head, he walked up the street towards Reeves' home.

When he was only four doors away, he heard the first police sirens in the distance. He cursed. He'd thought he had made it undetected, but there was a chance it was him the cops were coming for. He ran to Reeves' building and buzzed his apartment. If he could get inside before the law arrived, there was a chance he'd avoid them.

The intercom crackled. "Who is it?"

"Herron."

There was a long pause. "Go away. Our business is done."

Herron knew he should have tailgated another of the building's residents inside and just show up on Reeves' doorstep. It was harder to talk back when you had a pistol in your face. The sirens were getting louder now, and he was getting more desperate. If he couldn't get inside in the next five seconds, he'd have to retreat to his motorbike and try to slip away. But if he couldn't secure Reeves' help, he couldn't find the Master.

He pressed the intercom button again. "You need to reconsider. Fast."

There was no response: Reeves was playing hard to get. Herron cursed and slammed his palm into the wall. He considered kicking in the glass door, but then the first cop car came tearing down the street. Herron walked back to his bike. With each step, he expected the police to pounce, but instead they drove right past him and pulled up in front of Reeves' apartment block.

Any chance of using the NSA analyst to get back on the Master's trail was now gone, but while he climbed back on the bike and started the engine, Herron didn't immediately ride away. He was too engrossed with what was happening outside the building, where four officers had emerged from the cars and were forcing their way inside.

Herron watched them disappear, only to return a few minutes later with Michael Reeves in handcuffs. The NSA analyst was dressed in his pyjamas and looked shocked, which wasn't surprising given that only a few minutes earlier it'd been Herron at his door. The cops bundled him inside a car and drove away.

Herron rode off in the opposite direction, forming a new plan on the fly. He had no idea what had led to Reeves' arrest, but it had to be related to his own escape from custody. Somehow, the cops had linked his takedown of the Enclave leadership with Reeves. Another door was now closed to him, and things were getting desperate. Herron was almost entirely without resources and the net was closing in.

He was alone and his luck was failing. He'd have to create his own.

5

HERRON GRUNTED as he threw his duffel bag over the chain-link fence with enough force to clear the barbed wire atop it. Though it made a bit of noise as it landed, the bag didn't trigger any sort of alarm or security lighting. Despite his penetration of their outer perimeter, the grounds of Secure Corporation remained shrouded in the inky black of early morning.

That made things easier.

It was one thing to talk your way into a hospital, but getting access to a secure server housed in a security company was an entirely different proposition. When attacking this kind of facility, Herron would usually want to study the schematics, stake out the building to determine its security features and maybe even try to cultivate an asset on the inside.

He had time for none of that. He'd only had the chance to visit a hardware store and do a lap of the facility on his bike before getting to work. He'd parked a block away, donned a balaclava and then headed to the section of fence at the rear of the facility. He didn't know how difficult getting inside would be, but he was as well prepared as he'd had time to be.

Herron gripped the only thing he'd kept from the duffel bag – the bolt cutters he'd bought from the hardware store with the rest of his supplies. Satisfied there was little security aside from the fence – no motion lights, sensors, dogs or alarms – he used the cutters to make a hole in the mesh. He tossed the cutters onto the ground, gripped the section he'd cut free, and pulled.

After one last look around, he maneuvered through the gap. He drew his pistol, picked up the duffel bag and walked in the direction of the squat building that stood like a sentinel in the center of the grounds. It was four stories tall and likely contained all sorts of treasure, but Herron was only interested in one piece – the security camera footage from the hospital.

It'd been easy enough to figure out where the footage was stored. Secure Corporation stickers had been all over the hospital, spruiking the company's work to keep the hospital safe. A simple Google search at an all-night internet café had given Herron all the information he needed to crack open their security like a drill through drywall. Although the company's business was security, their own facility was lacking.

It'd be fine against most threats, but Herron wasn't most threats.

Like an onion, Secure Corporation's protection had layers. Besides the unguarded perimeter fence, Herron's reconnaissance had revealed a single guard at a gatehouse and another inside a well-lit reception area at the front. He was certain there'd be internal cameras, secure doors and possibly even roving teams of guards – none of it would be sufficient to stop him.

He reached the rear of the building and pressed his back up against it. Though he'd scouted the building and was cloaked in darkness, he couldn't be totally sure that he hadn't missed something. He waited there with his pistol gripped tight, his senses on a razor's edge, and ready to explode into action if the situation demanded. A full five minutes ticked by and nothing happened. It was safe to move.

Herron made his way to the back of the building, where a heavy steel door with a pair of locks restricted his access. Normally, he would have selected his tools based on a thorough reconnaissance of the target, but he hadn't had that option this time. Instead he'd procured a wide range of cheap tools – from a set of bump keys to some traditional lockpicks – that would let him deal with most locks.

Thankfully, the door only had a pair of simple tumbler locks. Herron opened the duffel bag and dug through its contents. He found the bump keys and within a minute he'd dealt with both mechanisms. He pushed down on its handle and the door opened freely on its hinges. Herron stashed the keys back in his bag and entered the offices of Secure Corporation.

He closed the door behind him and dug a small flashlight from the bag. He turned it on and looked around. There appeared to be no internal security features at all. If he was a client of Secure Corporation, he'd be alarmed at how easily someone with the right motivation and tools could work his way inside. Hell, he hadn't even needed most of the gear he'd purchased.

Herron used the flashlight to guide him through the maze of darkened cubicles that seemed to dominate this level of the building. Some of the desks were neat, some were cluttered, but Herron only cared about one thing. He examined each for a split second, until he found a terminal with a sticky note attached to the screen. On the note, whoever worked at the computer had written their username and password.

Herron smiled. It never failed.

He took a seat and turned on the computer. When it booted, he entered the login and password and the computer accepted his credentials. He went exploring and he soon found his way to the security camera archives. Within a few minutes, Herron had located the hospital, the correct ward, the right camera and roughly the time of day when he'd interrupted the Master wheeling the other Enclave operative to the elevator.

At exactly 9:43 PM, the Master had looked right up at the camera.

"Got you." Herron smiled. "You're mine now, asshole."

Herron let go of the mouse and opened up the desk drawer. He found a USB flash drive, inserted it into the computer, then dragged the camera footage onto the drive. The file was large, so it would take several minutes to transfer. Herron stood, keeping alert. Being interrupted now by a roving security patrol wouldn't be ideal.

For the first time since he'd left the rooftop in the helicopter, something went right for Herron. Nobody interrupted him as the transfer took place, and when it was completed he pulled the stick from the computer and put it in his pocket. Then he simply walked out of the office, across the grounds and out through the hole in the fence.

Herron rode his motorbike down the sleepy suburban street, counting down the numbers until he came to the modest, single-level house he was looking for. He stopped across the street and waited.

Even though it was 5:00 AM, after the experience at Reeves' apartment, he wanted to take a minute to make sure no cops appeared to spoil the party.

After one last look up and down the street, Herron killed the engine, kicked the stand and climbed off the bike. He crossed the street and walked up the driveway to Robert Graham's front door. Graham was one of the few people who could take the footage Herron had stolen and use it to unlock the Master's whereabouts.

When he reached the front door, Herron used the bump key he'd purchased from the hardware store to open it. The lock gave way in only a few seconds. After drawing his pistol, Herron eased the door open. A lamp was on in the living room, so he started there. He walked a few steps down the hallway, turned into the living room and was confronted by an overweight, middle-aged man asleep in an arm chair.

Still wearing the motorbike helmet and with his pistol aimed at the sleeping man, Herron crossed the room to the armchair. He kicked the sleeping man's leg. The sleeping giant snorted as he woke, his eyes locking onto Herron in a second. The man Herron assumed was Graham stared down the barrel of the pistol.

"You've made a terrible decision." Graham's voice was calm, despite the situation. "Who are you?"

"You're Robert Graham?" Herron waited until the other man nodded. "Great. We need to talk."

With Reeves off the board, Herron had lost the best way to track down the Master. The security camera footage he had stolen was useless without access to the FBI's Next Generation Identification-Interstate Photo System. It had over 400 million photos on file and was patched into camera feeds all across the country. It could also be accessed by Federal, state and local law enforcement all over the country.

Reeves could have accessed the system in a split second but now Herron had to work harder. He'd targeted the weakest link in the chain – Graham. The chief could access the system without suspicion, if given incentive to do so. Luckily, Herron was good at motivating people and he now had the police chief of a small county just outside of Washington D.C. at his mercy.

"I'll keep this simple." Herron spoke each word slowly, because he didn't want his captive to make a mistake. "I'm going to take my helmet off. Then I'm going to explain what you need to do. Then I'm going to put the pistol in my pocket. Then we're going to get your wife and two children. Then we're going to bring them into this room."

Graham's eyes were locked onto Herron now. "I—"

"I'm not finished." Herron cut him off. "Nobody needs to see the gun, unless you give me reason to. I don't want to frighten your kids, but I need you and your wife to do as I ask."

Graham nodded. Like most people, his professional façade had crumbled when his family was threatened. "And what is that exactly?"

Herron smiled. He had no intention of hurting the police chief's family, but Graham didn't know that. The illusion was all that mattered and there was one dead set way to create it. He removed his helmet and Graham's eyes looked between Herron's face and the pistol. Herron was glad Graham didn't seem to recognize who he was, because it meant he still had a chance to evade the authorities.

Herron clicked his fingers, so Graham paid attention. "I've killed a bunch of people. I want you to find a man for me. If you do so, I won't need to kill your family."

Graham nodded. "Tell me what you want."

Herron tossed the USB at Graham. The other man caught it. "I want you to find a man for me. The footage on that stick will help you do so."

"Is he in town?"

"I doubt it." Herron shrugged. "You need to use the Interstate Photo System. Find him and I'll leave your family in peace. You've got two hours before people start to die."

"Okay." Graham seemed to believe him. He showed no signs of resistance and nodded vigorously. "Just take it easy."

Herron stood, gestured for Graham to do likewise and followed him to the master bedroom. Herron put the pistol in his pocket, but kept his hand wrapped around the grip. When he nodded at Graham, the police chief entered the room and stood next to the bed. Herron flicked on the light and Graham's wife sat up in alarm. She glanced at her husband in confusion and then locked eyes with the intruder.

Graham covered his wife's mouth before she could scream. "Cara, it's okay, but you need to remain calm."

Herron gripped the pistol a little tighter as her eyes darted between Herron and her husband, but eventually she nodded. Graham sat down on the bed next to his wife and slowly removed his hand from her mouth. Herron was prepared for her to scream, but to her credit she kept quiet. She clearly recognized the danger and trusted her husband to navigate them back to safety.

"What's going on?" Cara Graham whispered. "Who is this man?"

Herron cut Graham's answer off. "I'm going to stay here with you and your children while your husband completes a task for me. If you stay calm and he co-operates, everybody stays safe."

Herron waited until she'd nodded her understanding and then gestured both of them out of the room. He followed them to the end of the house, where the children slept. A quick web search had revealed that Graham had two children – a boy and a girl – which were a key reason why he'd picked this cop to squeeze. Each child had their own bedroom, one next to the other. Herron waited outside while their parents split, each going to grab a child.

Neither Graham or his wife did anything stupid, which wasn't surprising given the stakes. They emerged from the bedrooms within a few seconds of each other, both hugging tired and confused children. Herron kept back as they all made for the living room and sat down on the sofa. The children were bleary-eyed and when their mother sat in between them, they soon fell back to sleep on her.

Herron walked to the kitchen that adjoined the living room and gestured for Graham to follow. He stood in the doorway between the rooms and waited while Graham moved past him and into the kitchen. From here, he could speak to the cop privately and also keep his eye on the man's family. He was still ready for Graham to try something – to rush him or try for a weapon – but for now he was staying compliant.

"Knock on the door when you get back. If I see cops or you don't cooperate fully, people die." Herron looked down at his watch and then back up at Graham. "Two hours.

* * *

"Go to jail! Go to jail!"

Given the events of the last few days, Herron laughed at the irony as the two children shouted at him in unison. Since Graham had left to complete his task, the kids had gradually woken up. They'd sat awkwardly with Herron and their mother for a little bit, before he had suggested they play a board game. He'd permitted the youngest child – the girl – to leave the living room and she'd returned with *Monopoly*.

He was letting the kids win and they'd become very animated when he'd landed on the tile that'd send him to the clink. The kids hollered and laughed as he moved his piece – the cannon – to the other side of the board and into the jail. Herron smiled at them and glanced at Cara Graham. She was sitting with her arms crossed, playing the game only to keep the peace. The kids were oblivious to her dark mood, but Herron was wary of it.

"Your turn." Herron stared at her, making it clear that she should continue with the game and the illusion of normalcy. "The kids are having a good time."

She faked a smile, which was laced with disdain and hatred. Though she rolled the dice and moved her piece forward, she showed no interest in purchasing the property she'd landed on. Herron kept his eyes on her as the children completed their turns, assessing whether or not she'd do something stupid. He had enough risk with Robert Graham. He wouldn't tolerate misbehavior from the man's wife.

The police chief had been gone for an hour and a half. His time was running out fast. By now, Herron hoped, he was finishing up his work and returning home. If not, there might be a problem. Though there was some chance that Graham would surround his house with cops, Herron doubted it. Not when there was a man in his living room holding his wife and kids hostage.

Of course, he wouldn't harm Cara Graham or the

kids if the cops did show up, but neither Graham nor his wife knew that.

Herron smiled at the children. "Hey kids, why don't you go into the kitchen and get us some soda and snacks?"

The kids looked at their mother. When she nodded, they shot off into the kitchen to collect their treasure.

Herron watched them leave, unworried about them being in there on their own. They'd been calm while playing the board game and he didn't think they knew he was a threat. Besides, he could accept that minor amount of risk, because doing so let him deal with a more significant potential problem.

He stared at Cara Graham. "I can see what you're doing. You're emotionally withdrawing, calculating the odds of taking me down or distracting me long enough for your kids to escape. You need to stop it. If your husband returns with what I need, everyone lives. If you interfere in the meantime, we have a big problem and neither of us will get what we want."

"I don't give a fuck what you want." She hissed. "If you touch either of my children I'll cut you in half."

Herron nodded at her as the kids returned to the living room. They'd reached an uneasy understanding: he wouldn't harm the children and she'd behave. She smiled at the two children and held her arms wide as they ran to her, laughing as they carried cans of soda and bags of candy into the room. They squealed with joy as they jumped into their mother's arms, showing her their haul.

The board games continued for another fifteen minutes. Herron started to grow anxious, checking his watch every few minutes while waiting for Robert Graham's return. He hadn't seriously considered a scenario where the police chief didn't return, but the man's wife clearly had. She was staring at Herron and seemed genuinely worried, even as she pretended to be fully engaged with the game.

The clock ticked down, until there were just two minutes left on Graham's deadline. Herron had given up on all illusion of playing the game now, digging his hand into his pocket and gripping the pistol. Two minutes ticked down to one, then down to thirty seconds. Herron sighed. He'd given Graham enough time to get what he needed to save his family, but it seemed the man hadn't delivered.

Things were about to get complicated.

Herron locked eyes with Cara Graham. While her children continued to play the game, she was silently pleading with Herron to leave the children alone. He kept his face impassive. He had to maintain the illusion of the threat, though he had no idea what he was going to do if the police chief didn't deliver. He wouldn't harm the family, but he needed help to find the Master.

There was a knock on the door with four seconds to spare. Herron glanced at Cara Graham. The relief on her face was plain to see. She moved off the sofa and sat down next to her children, ostensibly to wrap them both in a hug. It was clear to Herron that she was also preparing to shield them with her own body if the situation became violent. He doubted it would, not unless the local SWAT team was dumb enough to knock.

"Hopefully this is the last time I'll see you." Herron looked at Cara Graham as he stood. "Have fun, kids!"

He walked through the house to the front door, his hand in his pocket gripping the pistol. At the front door, he looked through the peephole. Robert Graham was on the other side, holding both of his hands in the air so Herron could see. One was empty and the other held a folder.

Herron opened the door. He wasn't going to deny Graham access to his family for a second longer than necessary, once he had his information. "Good timing."

"I got what you wanted." Graham held out the folder. It was stuffed with paper. "Several hits, including one from yesterday.

Herron nodded, took the folder and opened it. He skimmed through the contents and was satisfied Graham had delivered. He looked up at Graham. "And nobody suspects you?"

"No."

"Good. Your wife is a strong woman." Herron stood aside and let Graham pass. He was a man of his word.

Herron waited until Graham was out of site, then left the house. He looked up and down the street, but only a few cars were on the road. It was almost as sleepy as when he'd arrived. It was still relatively early and most people would only now be getting ready for work. Herron had to get ready for work, too. He had a lot of catching up to do and a long ride ahead of him.

It was a long way to Mexico.

6

"COME ON." Herron's eyes flared as he slowed the car to a stop. The traffic had to be backed up for a mile.

He tapped the wheel in tune with the song on the radio, until the music was overwhelmed by music blaring from a car that pulled up next to him. He turned to stare at the two men in the front seat. They were covered in jewellery and tattoos – probably gangbangers – and like Herron they were headed for the border with Mexico.

Herron stifled a yawn. He was tired, but he didn't dare stop moving. Not when he was this close.

After leaving Graham's house he'd headed south. He'd stayed on the motorbike until he'd hit Texas, where he'd accessed one of his stashes, collecting cash and a new fake identity. After sleeping at a hotel, he'd then stolen a car before continuing south to the Mexican border. After 14 hours, stopping only for gas and food a few times along the way, he was at one of several U.S./Mexico border checkpoints.

The traffic was moving nowhere fast, so Herron reached over to the passenger seat and grabbed the folder Graham had given him. He'd already perused the papers in detail at a gas station diner. They contained countless photos of the Master, several identities the Enclave leader had used and financial records for many of those identities.

Most of that was noise. What really mattered was a still photograph taken from a security camera recording at Dulles International Airport that showed the Master boarding a flight to Europe two days ago.

The Master had fled the United States and Herron was following. It was getting too hot to stay here anyway, with law enforcement all over the country scouring their jurisdictions to find him. While finding the Master in Europe would be like finding a needle in a haystack in a field full of haystacks, at least Herron would be able to get away from some of the attention that was currently on him.

He was a few pages into the dossier when the traffic started to move again. He closed the folder and put it back on the passenger seat, then inched the car forward a few yards before the traffic stopped again. Ahead of him was a sea of red tail lights, each belonging to a car carrying a frustrated motorist or family south. He'd been moving at this pace for over an hour.

By now he could read the LED message board

above the checkpoint up ahead. It explained why the traffic was so bad: the authorities were completing enhanced vehicle searches. Herron cursed. He hadn't expected to cross the border easily, but he'd hoped his disguise and fake passport would be enough. With the border guards on higher alert, he couldn't count on it.

As his car crawled forward, Herron adjusted to the situation. He formed a plan and kept his eyes peeled. He was looking for something very specific – a perfect set of circumstances that would let him depart the United States unmolested, despite the enhanced security checks up ahead. He was on the clock. He needed to find what he was looking for before he reached the checkpoint.

Herron looked to his left at the sedan the gangbangers were driving. This time, the man in the passenger seat looked at him. Herron smiled. "The music is a little loud."

The thug hissed. "Keep staring at me. We might add the sound of your head slamming into my fist."

Herron almost laughed at the thought of these guys trying to dish out violence near one of the most hotly policed checkpoints on the planet, but he kept quiet. He gripped the wheel tighter with both hands and looked straight ahead, back into the sea of red lights. His antagonist hurled more abuse at him, trying to spark a reaction, but soon lost interest when Herron didn't respond.

Herron had made his decision. Though he didn't usually target innocents, he doubted that description fit these guys. At best, they were assholes.

He gripped his pistol and ejected the magazine into his lap, then wound down the electric window on the front passenger side and tossed the gun out into the darkness. Unless someone was watching his car very closely, they wouldn't have noticed what he was doing. Satisfied nobody had noticed, next he emptied the magazine and tossed that out the window too.

He gathered the bullets in a small pile on his lap and waited. The next time the traffic moved, Herron only pulled forward a little way. Now, instead of being alongside him, the gangbangers' Chevrolet was slightly in front, the back windows down and their music pumping. Herron pinched the first of the bullets between his thumb and forefinger and threw it through the back window of the gangbangers' car.

His aim was true and the bullet went through the window.

Herron waited to see if there'd be any reaction from the men inside the car, but their music was so loud they were oblivious to his actions. He repeated the move over and over again, until each of the bullets he'd taken from inside the pistol was on the back seat of the gangbanger's car. Only then did he close the distance between his vehicle and the car in front, pulling up alongside the Chevrolet again.

The traffic snailed along for another 15 minutes, and as he got closer Herron could see that the officers at the border checkpoint were thoroughly searching every car. Off to the side, were several empty cars – their occupants must have failed the inspection and were probably getting some extra attention somewhere. He pulled up at the border checkpoint at the same time as the Chevrolet, hoping his plan worked.

The officer policing Herron's lane leaned down to look through the window. "Good evening, sir. I'll need to see your identification."

Herron nodded and made a show of rifling through his glove compartment. Every few seconds, he glanced up and mouthed some words of apology, but he was really waiting for the officer in the next lane over to create a stink about the bullets in the back of the gangbangers' vehicle. Worrying it was taking too long, he produced his fake passport and handed it over.

"About time." The border guard took the passport from Herron. He looked at the identification and then at Herron. "New look, sir?"

Herron had been prepared for the question. The photo in his fake passport had a lot more hair than he currently did. He shrugged. "Time catches up with all of us."

"It sure does. I—"

The officer stopped speaking; something was happening behind him. A commotion had broken out in the next lane over, where his colleague had been inspecting the gangbangers' car. They still hadn't turned down the music. Combined with their face tattoos and generally unfriendly demeanor, they were getting more attention than most other motorists.

Herron was counting on it.

The officer inspecting their car had flashed his flashlight into the back of their car and all hell had broken loose. He stepped back and drew his pistol, screaming at the gangbangers to freeze and for his colleagues to assist him. For their part, the gangbangers just looked angry and confused. Herron smiled when he saw the official inspecting his car reach for his own pistol and turn to help his colleague.

Herron raised his voice a little. "Can I go now, officer?"

The man holding Herron's fake passport looked back at him, but was still distracted by the drama in the other lane. He nodded, handed back the passport and waved him through. Herron watched for another second, more out of pleasure than any need to stick around. The guard who'd searched his car joined his colleague in the next lane over, adding to the commotion. The gangbangers were going to have a bad day.

Herron laughed as he hit the gas.

* * *

Herron exhaled loudly as he stepped off the bus and onto the sidewalk out front of Mexico City International Airport. He took a few steps away from the bus, paused and took in his surroundings. Though the airport was pulsating with activity as passengers hauled luggage all around him, he had no sense that anything was off. He hefted his backpack and entered the terminal.

After clearing the border from the United States, he'd driven direct to Mexico City and parked the car in the middle of the street. He'd left the doors unlocked and the engine running; confident the Mexican underworld would take care of the car and doubting it would ever be seen again. Without wheels of his own now, he'd caught the bus to the airport. Arriving there felt like home.

Mexico City International Airport was the busiest airport in Latin America. Every day, 100,000 passengers passed through it, travelling to and from more than 100 destinations. An airport serving that many travellers perfectly suited Herron's purposes, because it had enough scale that he could exploit the many cracks in its security. He'd relied on that fact plenty of times during his career with the Enclave and now he was relying on it again.

He whistled softly to himself as he walked through the terminal to the Aero Mexico ticket counter. On the way, he exchanged a few thousand U.S. Dollars for a whole lot more Mexican pesos, which he'd need to cover the price of the airline ticket. When he reached the counter of the Mexican national carrier, he only had to wait a few moments before a ticket agent called him forward.

"Hello." Herron smiled at the female staff

member manning the desk. "I'd like to buy a ticket to Paris, leaving as soon as possible."

"Let me see what I can find." The attendant looked down at her computer and started to type. A second later, she looked back up at him. "There's a flight in four hours."

"Perfect." Herron put his passport and a large number of pesos on the counter in front of the attendant. "That should cover it?"

"Yes, sir." She took possession of his passport, opened the document to the photo page and put it face-down on her scanner. "This will just take a moment."

"No problem." Herron's easy demeanor masked the ice that was running through his veins. Everything counted on his false identification passing this test.

"Okay." She handed back the passport and processed the payment for the ticket, then handed him a receipt. "There you go, sir."

He walked away from the counter, glad to be over the first hurdle. The true test was ahead of him at security. Though his passport hadn't triggered any alarms, there was no telling if some attentive security guard had seen his photo on the news or a law enforcement alert system.

Fortunately, he had a secret weapon.

Herron approached the security checkpoint and stopped short of it. He took a second to look at the guards on each of the metal detectors and bag scanners. While there was a good chance he'd get through, he wanted to guarantee it, so picked the line that maximized his odds. It shuffled forward slowly, until Herron was close enough to put his bag on the belt of the scanner and step up to the metal detector.

Though the metal detector didn't make a sound as he passed through it, the guard didn't give Herron permission to proceed. As he'd feared, the guard was summing him up. He stared at Herron and then glanced around, possibly looking for a supervisor. Herron's papers were perfect, but they were meant to help him survive when there was no scrutiny on him. The best papers in the world wouldn't help him if the guards were looking for him.

As he stood at the metal detector, Herron's mind was screaming at him to act – to run or unleash violence – but Herron ignored the impulse. Instead, he turned his attention to the guard at the bag scanner. He was an older man – about fifty or so – and looked like the world had weighed heavy on him. He was leaning back in his chair with his arms crossed, not paying too much attention to the bags he was responsible for inspecting.

Until Herron's bag appeared on the screen and his eyes widened. A million dollars in cash appearing on your screen had that effect.

Herron smiled at the guard as the other man turned away from the screen and locked eyes on him. The guard stopped the conveyer belt, stood and walked over to his colleague on the metal detector. After some urgent whispering, both guards walked back to the conveyer belt and opened Herron's bag.

To their credit, they kept their cool, not revealing to anyone else that they had almost a million dollars at their fingertips.

Herron was still standing a few steps past the metal detector, watching the guards. When they both turned to stare at him, he nodded and raised an eyebrow. So much was communicated without speaking, but Herron already knew the answer to his question. In a country where the average worker earned five bucks a day, a million of them was a life-changing proposition.

"You can go." The older guard at the bag scanner pointed at Herron. "Safe travels."

Herron turned and headed for his gate.

* * *

Herron's eyes flickered open and he blinked in confusion as the captain of the aircraft announced they were preparing for landing. Was it possible that he'd slept for the entire flight, all the way to Charles De Gaulle International Airport in Paris? It was the first time Herron had slept uninterrupted by a nightmare in almost 10 years.

He rubbed his face and sat up in his seat. It was no surprise he'd been so tired, because he'd pushed himself hard for the three days prior to boarding the flight. Now his body was rested, he could think more clearly as well. He was glad to finally be out of the U.S. Though his profile would have been beamed the world over, he doubted authorities in France and the rest of Europe would be quite so vigilant in pursuing him.

That would give him more freedom to act.

The hard part would be finding the Master. Herron knew his target had flown in two days ago, but as that information became less current he risked losing the trail again. Europe was a big continent and there were lots of places to hide. Though the Master had far fewer resources at his disposal after Herron had gutted the Enclave leadership and flushed him from his home country, he was still a dangerous foe.

Once Herron was off the plane and clear of airport security, he could disappear back into the shadows. Though he had fewer resources of his own in Europe and didn't know its underbelly as well as America's, that also offered certain advantages. Europe didn't know him, either. He was a wild card without an employer or a reputation, on a continent he hadn't visited in five years.

The plane touched down, the pilot taxied to the terminal, the seatbelt light turned off and the frenzy began. People jostled for their bags and for space in the aisle, and a few minutes after the flight had pulled up to the gate, the doors opened. The passengers started to disembark, but Herron simply grabbed the folder from the seatback and waited for his turn to leave the plane.

Once inside the terminal, he knew he was being watched by dozens of cameras. He kept his head down as he walked slowly and calmly towards immigration, where he joined the line for processing. This was the last organized security checkpoint before he could cut loose in the expanses of Europe and get back on the trail of the Master. The line shuffled forward and eventually a young female officer waved him over.

"Bonjour." Herron smiled at the woman as he dug his passport out of his pocket and placed it on the counter.

"Bonjour." Her face was neutral as she scooped up the identification and opened it. As she flicked through the pages, she frowned and looked up at him. "Only one stamp?"

"I don't travel much." Herron shrugged. "My mother just died and her dream was to go to Paris. She never made it, so I told myself it was time to travel the world."

"I'm sorry for your loss." Her features lightened in sympathy as she stamped his passport. "Enjoy your time in Paris."

"Thanks."

Herron scooped up his documentation and continued on through the airport. The hard part was over, but he wouldn't relax until he was in the back of a cab. Now clear of immigration, he made his way to the baggage claim and waited for the bags to start their journey on the carousel. Though he hadn't checked any bags himself, nothing looked more suspicious to security than getting off a one-way, long-haul flight with no luggage.

Herron stood near the mouth of the carousel,

where the bags came out first, and plucked a red suitcase at random. He waited for a few moments, to make sure nobody would take issue, then wheeled the suitcase through customs and made it to the exit. The moment he stepped outside, he closed his eyes and filled his lungs with crisp morning air. He'd made it. Now he was safely on European soil, he was confident he could vanish.

Herron headed for the taxi area. The airport wasn't busy, so he was inside a cab in less than two minutes. As they left the pickup area and pulled onto the highway, Herron started making small talk with the cabbie, a man who spoke perfect French and English. In his experience, the taxi drivers always knew where to find trouble. And trouble was exactly what he was looking for.

He was about to become a predator again.

7

HERRON SAT on a park bench and sipped his coffee, watching the townhouse at the end of the row. The cabbie had recommended the place when Herron had enquired about buying drugs. He wasn't actually planning to buy any, but he needed cash and weapons and knew one sure-fire trick to get them. But before performing that trick, he'd wanted to know what he was in for.

In the time he'd been sitting there, he'd seen four separate cars pull up in front of the townhouse. The people in the cars never climbed out. They simply waited. A teenager would emerge from the alley that ran alongside the townhouse, run to the waiting car, make a quick exchange and return to hiding. It was as regular as clockwork.

Herron stood, crossed the street and entered the alleyway. There was a car parked there – an upmarket BMW in a decidedly downmarket part of town. The combination of the exchanges out front and the fancy car out back told the whole story. There may as well have been a neon sign advertising the drug house, and Herron had no problem preying on criminals to get what he needed.

He leaned down to pick up a large rock from the ground, walked up to the BMW and slammed the rock into the driver's-side window.

The glass shattered and an alarm wailed.

Herron dropped the rock and leaned against the car. Within seconds, the back door of the townhouse flew open and two men emerged – one was the teenager from earlier and the other a man in his mid-thirties hefting a baseball bat. The older man was fit and Herron guessed he was the enforcer. Both men stared at the car for a second and then started shouting at him in French.

Herron didn't speak French, so he let his actions do the talking. After taking one last sip from his coffee cup, he removed the lid and tossed it through the broken window. The remains of the coffee spilled over the leather seats, the floor and the dashboard.

Enraged, the thugs advanced on him. The enforcer with the bat led the way – Herron would be happy to wipe the floor with him, because he was an adult whose dumb choices were his own responsibility. The kid was a different story. Herron didn't want to hurt him, but was sure witnessing extreme violence inflicted on someone else would make him crumble.

Herron took a step forward as the thug wound up

and swung the bat at his head. As it whizzed closer, he ducked under its arc and struck like a viper. He gripped his attacker's left wrist, twisted it and broke it. The older man screamed, and Herron let go of the wrist and caught the bat. He lashed out with all the force he could and slammed it into the enforcer's jaw, sending him sprawling to the ground.

Herron planted his foot on the thug's chest and fixed the teenager with a hard stare.

The boy turned and ran out of the alley.

Herron watched the kid until he was out of sight, then looked down at the enforcer. He was crying in pain as he cradled his broken wrist. "What to do with you?"

"Fuck you!" The thug's voice was high with pain.

Herron paused, taken aback. "You speak English?"

The injured man glared at him defiantly.

"The fucking French" Herron frisked the man for weapons and found none. "Go."

Herron stepped off the thug. The man got to his feet and staggered away, leaving the door to the drug house open wide behind him. Herron moved inside, checking each room and ready to unleash violence on anyone in his way. Everything was clear until he came across a man passed out on the sofa. He was probably the boss of the crew, who'd left his minions to do the work while he slept.

Herron gripped the dealer by the throat. When the man's eyes shot open, Herron leaned down until his face was inches from the dealer's. "Speak English?"

"Who...fuck are you?" The dealer's voice was broken and raspy from the pressure on his throat. "You're...dead man!"

"Threats aren't the way to greet a man who can crush your windpipe." Herron squeezed tighter. "Where do you keep the money and the guns?"

Panic set in on the dealer's face, his eyes bulging as he tried to fight back. He punched and kicked, then pried at Herron's fingers – nothing worked. Herron fended off the blows easily. Finally, the dealer pointed across the room in the direction of the television.

Herron loosened his grip. "Where?"

The dealer inhaled sharply and coughed. "TV cabinet."

Herron stood to his full height. "If you're lying or if you move, I'll tear you in half."

Keeping one eye on the dealer, he crossed the room and searched through the three drawers. As promised, he found treasure – drugs, cash, several pistols and a sawed-off shotgun. There was also an old backpack and Herron stuffed a large number of Euros and a few of the guns inside it. Then he took out the drawer with the drugs and carried it across the living room to the kitchen.

He wouldn't leave the poison for the dealer to sell.

"No! Please!" The dealer's voice was filled with panic as he realized what Herron was doing. "They'll kill me!"

Herron enjoyed the terror on the man's face – he'd probably brought misery to thousands, and now he was about to experience some of his own. He aimed the sawed-off at the dealer, ran water into the sink and poured the drugs out of their little bags. He started with the powder and followed up with the pills. In seconds, the dealer's stock was a soggy mess in the sink.

Herron hefted the backpack and kept the shotgun trained on the criminal. "Tell me where you get the stuff from."

* * *

Herron revelled in the performance of the BMW as he accelerated down the street. Even the overwhelming smell of coffee didn't bother him; the smashed window had helped to air it out. He'd cleared out the shattered glass as best as he could, to make it seem he just had the window wound down. The last thing he needed was a nosy cop seeing a broken window and asking questions.

Slowing as he entered the industrial precinct, Herron scanned the numbers on the warehouses until he found the address the dealer had given him. He stopped the car out front and appraised the building. Past the high fences and the solid-looking gate, the front of the warehouse was dominated by a large roller-door. There were no signs on the building or on the white van parked out front, which increased the chances of finding something illicit.

The drug house had been easy to crack. It was an outpost, likely one of dozens of smaller fiefdoms controlled by two-bit dealers. They were supplied by and paid tribute to a warlord, and if the dealer had told him the truth, the warehouse Herron was looking at was the control center for the operation. Though it didn't look like it from the outside, it would likely be more strongly guarded than the townhouse.

There was one way to find out.

Herron lined the rear of his vehicle up with the main gate, shifted the car into reverse and floored it. The BMW shot backwards with an impressive amount of power and Herron grunted a second later when it slammed into the gate. He shifted into drive, moved the damaged car forward and repeated the process until the obstruction gave way.

He opened the door and climbed out of the car. Though the rear of the vehicle was totaled and the gate had held up better than he'd thought, it had yielded. He pulled his pistol from the waistband of his jeans, reached inside the car for the sawed-off shotgun, stepped over the fallen gate and made his way to the warehouse.

At the door, he fired the sawed-off into the handle. Buckshot shredded the handle and the lock. He dropped the shotgun, kicked the door open and moved inside with his pistol leveled. Gunfire greeted him. Herron scrambled for the nearest available cover – a stack of building materials – as shots hammered into the steel frame around the door.

He waited for a few seconds, letting the shooters burn their ammo firing at a target who was safely behind heavy cover. He used the time to assess the situation. There were large stacks of construction supplies all across the warehouse floor, each about ten-feet high. Above him, three shooters armed with pistols were firing down from a gantry that ringed the warehouse and also cut through the middle of it.

Herron had faced worse odds.

Still huddling behind cover, he used the sound of the gunfire to roughly map the position of the shooters on the gantry: two were dead ahead and one was more to the left – he was the main threat. Herron aimed the pistol up and to his left, waiting for the shooter to inch around and try to get a shot off. He didn't have to wait long. The gunman appeared, Herron fired and his target dropped with a scream.

With the threat on his flank dealt with, Herron could get more aggressive. He waited until there was a lull in the gunfire and then emerged from cover. The two remaining assailants were standing close together on the walkway, with no cover to protect them. Though they fired at Herron, their aim was poor. Herron had no such problem: he dropped each target with a single shot.

He scanned for more attackers, but the cavernous building had gone quiet except for the screams of a wounded shooter. He was sure there'd be more criminals operating from this warehouse, but it seemed only three were present now. He swapped out his pistol magazine and climbed the stairs to the second level. He needed to end this quickly and get out. There was no telling when others might arrive.

The two gunmen who'd been ahead of him were dead. Herron mentally sounded off his 156th and 157th kills and then moved around to the wounded guy – the one who'd tried to flank him. He wasn't in great shape. The buckshot had pierced him in multiple places and he was bleeding out. Herron aimed his pistol down at the pusher.

The Frenchman gasped. "Putain! Va te faire enculer!"

"Uh-uh. English. Who's in charge here?"

"Me!"

"Wrong." Herron fired two shots into the pusher's head. "158."

He searched the bodies, turning up a box of matches and a set of keys for the van outside. He pocketed the matches and the keys, then made his way through the warehouse until he found where the drugs were manufactured and stored. This was an operation on an industrial scale, which supplied the smaller outposts like the one he had busted open at the townhouse. He also found more guns and millions of Euros sorted into brick-sized stacks.

Herron stuffed all of the cash into plastic bags and carried them to the front of the warehouse, where he loaded them into the back of the van. It took several trips, plus one last run back inside to sift through the firearms. He settled on a better-quality pistol and a submachine gun. Now he had all the resources he needed to take down the Master.

Before that, he had one last job to do.

The production of illicit drugs like heroin, methamphetamines and all the other kinds of pills and powders in the warehouse required a large amount of flammable chemicals. He located some drums and containers of combustible liquids and poured them all over the production area and building supplies, leaving a trail of fluid behind him as he made his way outside. Then he lit a match and threw it onto the ground.

As the line of flame leapt back to the warehouse, Herron turned and walked away.

* * *

Herron kept alert as he headed to his third strip club for the afternoon – for business, not pleasure. He'd parked the van at a parking garage and, although he was nervous about leaving millions of Euros unguarded, he had little choice. He was looking for someone, and the places he needed to check didn't usually offer parking for customers. He just had to hope nobody found the van.

As he entered the club, pulsating dance music with a deep bassline pounded his senses, the soundtrack to the two near-naked women gyrating around poles on a stage. A bar ran the length of one wall, with private booths along the opposite one, and there were chairs close to the stage and tables a little further out. None of them were occupied by the people Herron was searching for.

Had he struck out again?

He headed for the bar and ordered a Lagavulin – neat – which he nursed for an hour. He glanced at the strippers only occasionally; if he'd seen one stripper, he'd seen them all. A few of the girls working the floor tried to sell him a private lap dance, but he sent them packing. He liked a beautiful woman as much as the next guy but he was working, watching every arrival and departure from the club.

When three men entered wearing biker gang leathers, Herron knew he had the right place.

It was a universal truth that organized crime ran the brothels, the strip clubs and the drug trade. Whatever the local flavor, it didn't matter. Herron needed manpower, and taking down the local drug business at the warehouse was the first step to getting it. Because there hadn't been any signs the operation he'd destroyed had belonged to bikers, these guys would do fine.

The three stocky bikers took seats at the table furthest from the bar, right on the other side of the stage near the private rooms. Two were in their thirties and clearly subordinate to the third, who looked about fifty. Herron briefly wondered which gang they were from, but couldn't read the words on their club patch, which featured some sort of winged demon.

He drained his drink, pushed himself off the bar

and walked over to them. Their attention was locked on the latest pair of dancers and it wasn't until he was a few steps away that they peeled their eyes off the tits and ass. The two younger men looked at him like spiders surveying a bug stupid enough to fly into their web. The older biker just looked curious.

"Hey, fellas." Herron held his hands out wide as he stopped short of the table and tried the only French phrase he knew. "Parlez-vous anglais?"

They didn't respond. The biker leader simply gestured with his chin and one of his two compatriots stood. He was an ugly dude, with a shaved head and a fat face, but his body looked solid. He cracked his knuckles and advanced on Herron with violence in his eyes.

Herron laughed. He'd dealt with gangbangers at the Mexican border, then French drug dealers, and now outlaw bikers – he was taking down scumbags the world over.

"You sure you want to do this?" Herron sighed and raised his fists. He hadn't planned to fight them. "I just want to talk to you. Please, I want your help w—"

The biker took a swing. Herron jerked back and the roundhouse hit nothing but air. He fended off a few more amateur punches, then went in for the kill. When the biker threw a left, Herron stepped forward and to the side of the blow. Now inside his foe's guard, he delivered a brutal knee to the stomach and a jaw-breaking uppercut to his chin.

The thug's eyes went glassy and he dropped.

Herron stepped back from his downed foe and looked right past the other young biker, who'd just climbed to his feet. He kept his focus on the leader. "I just want to talk. You understand? Talk?"

The veteran held up a hand to stall his comrade, glanced at the downed man in disgust, then looked at Herron. "Oui, je comprends. Talk."

"You want control of the local drug trade?"

The biker raised an eyebrow. "Go on."

"The current owners went out of business." Herron reached into his pocket and held up the keys to the van. "This is for their van. It's full of their cash. Millions of Euros."

The older man gestured for the conscious biker to sit, then crossed his arms and fixed Herron with a hard stare. "And in return?"

Herron sat at the table. "I need help with someone."

"You want them killed?" The biker glanced down at his stunned foot soldier, who was just starting to stir. "It seems you need no help with this."

"I want someone found." Herron put the keys to the van back into his pocket. "Help me and the van is yours. Everything inside it too."

"You give us the keys and the van now." The biker's gaze was unwavering. "You tell the truth, we find your man."

Herron smiled. He wasn't stupid enough to give them their prize before the work was done. He did have a way to prove it, though. He dug into his other pocket, pulled out a thick wad of €500 notes, and threw the stack on the table. There must have been fifty grand in the stack, and Herron wanted to use it to buy access to the hundreds of members the biker gang would have across Europe.

"Proof enough?" He put out his hand. "I'm Herron."

"Yes." The biker shook it. "Pierre."

"I think we're going to be very good friends."

Pierre's English was far better than Herron's French, but it still took time for Herron to explain what he wanted in return for the money. He gave Pierre the location of every Enclave safehouse in Europe – the obvious places to start looking for the Master. Every safehouse was to be hit simultaneously by at least six heavily-armed bikers. Any that were found empty were to be burned to the ground.

Anyone the bikers discovered was to be restrained until Herron got there.

When the explanation was over, Pierre simply nodded and started work. He made dozens of calls, arranging for the other chapters of his gang in countries all across Europe to visit the addresses Herron had given him. Even if they were empty, Herron was taking them off the board as possible resources that the Master could use. While Pierre worked, Herron kept alert and drank Coke.

A few hours later, everything was ready. Pierre looked at Herron. "You are ready?"

"Do it."

Pierre nodded and shot off a group text message. The minutes ticked by excruciatingly slowly then, one by one, Pierre heard back from his breach teams. As the number of negative reports increased, Herron's mood darkened. It looked like he was going to come up empty, until Pierre checked in with the last team and everything changed.

Pierre looked at Herron. "The team in Amsterdam, they have found someone. A woman. They have her, but first she killed one of my men."

"Tell your team to hold her until we get there." Herron downed the last of his Coke and stood. "Time to go."

8

"This is the place." Pierre had to raise his voice to be heard over the sound of the motorcycles idling outside the Amsterdam townhouse. They'd ridden direct from Paris.

Herron looked at Pierre, his borrowed Harley still rumbling beneath him. "You come with me. Your men can stay out here, yes?"

"Yes."

Herron climbed off his bike and followed Pierre inside. They walked through to the living room, where the bikers who'd raided this safehouse were guarding their prisoner. She was tied up with a pillowcase over her head, but Herron could feel the threat emanating from her.

"Ask them what happened."

Before Pierre could speak, one of the bikers stepped forward. "I speak English."

"Okay." Herron shrugged. "You tell me."

The biker shrugged. "We thought the place was clear..."

"Then I slit the throat of your friend." The woman laughed from beneath the hood.

Herron admired her chutzpah. She hadn't realized that a former Enclave operative was in the house. It was time for her to find out who was really in charge. He stepped closer to her and removed the pillowcase from her head. She blinked quickly to adjust to the light. She was in her mid-thirties, with her auburn hair tied into a high ponytail and wearing black from head to toe.

She looked at Herron like a snake looks at a fieldmouse. "You shouldn't have come here. You're going to die."

"I was searching for the Master, but you'll do."

Her face scrunched up in contempt. "Do you really think he'd be stupid enough to come to a safehouse you know the location of?"

"Why not? I've wiped out the Enclave's leadership and he's on the run. He has no other resources."

"Is that what you think?" She laughed. "He didn't come to Europe to run away from you. He came to reboot the Enclave."

She had to be lying, trying to make him mad or force a mistake. The Enclave had been toppled and there was no way to put back the struts he and Jessica had kicked out. Every handler in North America had been shot dead. The organization had been totally decapitated.

Except for one man. But could that one man bring all the whole Enclave back?

"Pardon," Pierre interrupted Herron's train of thought. "We are done here."

Herron turned to see the biker veteran had a cell phone in one hand and a pistol in the other. The pistol was aimed at Herron. "We had a deal."

"It is true. But my men found your van in Paris." Pierre shrugged. "Now I have your money, you are both...how you say...the loose ends."

"Money? This is about money?" The woman looked at Pierre. "Free me and I can give you as much you like."

Herron shook his head. He cursed himself for not hiding the van better. He should have known the bikers would be searching high and low for it. "She's lying."

Pierre regarded her. "You are right, I think. She is...full of shit, n'est-ce pas?"

A heavy blow cracked the back of Herron's head. He grunted and started to fall, but Pierre's men grabbed his arms and stopped him. Herron fought, but it was no good – their grip was vice-like. One of them took the pistol from the back of his jeans while Pierre kept his own gun aimed at him.

"You are a dangerous man." Pierre shrugged. "Too dangerous, I think. You understand."

Herron did – Pierre had seen how ruthless he could be...what was to stop him treating Pierre like a 'loose end' too, once all this was over?

He kept quiet. He needed Pierre to move his

attention and his pistol elsewhere if he wanted to deal with the two bikers pinning his arms. After a moment, Pierre turned to the woman, aimed at her. He seemed disappointed when she didn't react; her eyes were black holes devoid of emotion. She was calm and ready to strike when she had the opportunity.

Pierre looked her up and down hungrily. Herron didn't need it spelled out, what the biker was thinking.

"I think you and I will be great friends." Pierre stepped in closer and kissed the woman on the lips. "I will keep you un petit moment, perhaps."

Pierre started to untie her, and Herron sprang into action. He stomped on the foot of the biker holding his left arm, loosening his grip enough for Herron to free his arm and elbow him in the nose. The injured man cried out and lifted his hands to his face, leaving Herron with only one captor to deal with.

The woman exploded from the chair and gripped Pierre by the throat, driving him back a few steps then ramming a knee into his testicles. He collapsed in a heap and she stepped over him, scooped up pistol and ran for the front door.

Herron moved to follow her – if he lost her now he'd be left with nothing – but the biker still holding onto him wasn't giving up, delivering a shot to his kidneys. Herron gripped the biker's hand and twisted. The thug tried to compensate by moving the rest of his body, but Herron turned the wrist in on itself until he heard a pop. He cut the biker's cry of pain short with a headbutt and let him slump to the ground.

Herron scooped up his pistol and then ran after the woman, knowing he might already be too late. Though he was less than 15 seconds behind, that was a lifetime against someone who was trained. He heard gunshots from outside and the roar of an engine.

When he reached the street, carnage confronted him. Three bikers were sprawled out in the road, blood pooling around them. In the distance, the woman was accelerating away on a stolen Harley.

"Fuck!"

Herron dug into his pocket for the keys to his bike, climbed on and started it. The engine responded with its distinctive *pop-pop-pause* rumble, and a second after he kicked up the stand he hit full throttle. The Harley roared underneath him and Herron gritted his teeth as it hit 55 MPH – breakneck speed in a city of canals, narrow roads and a whole lot of cyclists.

Bicycle bells and Dutch swear words echoed in his wake.

* * *

The townhouses of inner-urban Amsterdam gave

way to less dense housing, and the further the chase went from the city, the fewer cars there were to clog the roads. Herron rode fast and recklessly – testing the limits of his abilities – but he had no choice if he wanted to catch the woman. Chasing her east, they crossed the border from the Netherlands into Germany and hit an autobahn.

It wasn't long before they attracted the attention of a cop.

The police car sped in between him and his target, with sirens blaring and lights flashing. Herron had to strike. He pushed the bike harder and gained on the patrol car. When he was a few feet off the tail of the vehicle, Herron swerved the bike one lane over and pulled up alongside it. The cops eyed him curiously, but he'd deliberately chosen to pull up on the driver's side. The officer at the wheel wouldn't be able to draw his pistol and shoot.

Herron drew his own weapon from the waistband of his jeans. Hitting a moving target from a speeding bike would be difficult for most shooters, but then Mitch Herron wasn't most shooters. He unloaded his magazine into the hood of the car, shot after shot hammering into the engine. As sparks ricocheted off the hood's metalwork, the cop swerved into Herron's lane, trying to knock him down.

He turned the bike away from the swerving car as smoke started to billow from under its hood. The vehicle's speed bled away rapidly and the cops were out of the game, so he turned his attention back to his real target. He was going to catch this woman if it killed him, but after emptying his pistol into the cop car he was going to have to change his approach – he was out of ammo and she still had a loaded pistol.

Flashing past cars travelling at much lower speeds, he glanced down at the bike's instrument display. Soon, the light he'd been dreading flashed red on the panel. He had maybe 5 miles of gas left in the tank and after another few minutes, the fuel gauge hit empty. Herron cursed. There were no signs of the female operative running out of fuel, despite both bikes having been filled up at the same gas station in France.

His Harley gradually lost speed as the engine sucked up the final fumes in the tank, but to Herron's surprise, he wasn't losing any ground on his foe. She was out of gas as well.

Both bikes came to a stop less than 10 yards apart and Herron was the faster to draw his pistol and aim it at her. "Stay cool."

She hesitated then climbed off her bike and faced him with her hands held out wide. "Neat trick with the cop car."

Herron kept his weapon trained on her. "Take out your pistol and toss it on the road in front of me."

She nodded, drew her pistol and threw it onto the road. It skidded to a halt a few inches from his feet. Maintaining his aim, Herron reached down to secure her weapon, but the moment he looked away the woman was moving. Herron caught the motion in his peripheral vision and his instincts kicked in. He'd normally be able to shoot her, but he had no ammo.

He raised his guard, blocked her straight kick, but she landed a follow-up elbow to his temple. Herron grunted and staggered back, fending off the rain of blows by relying on instinct rather than skill. She lashed out with her elbow again – an identical strike to the one she'd initially landed – but Herron blocked it and delivered a quick jab to her chin. Though it didn't hit her hard, the shot caused her to back off a little.

He stepped back as she recovered from the blow. "I'm not interested in fighting you. I only want to find the Master."

"I don't know where he is. When my handler didn't answer my calls, I retreated to a safehouse. You know the protocol as well as I do."

Herron nodded. The first thing he'd been told as an Enclave operative was that his handler would always answer the phone. The second thing he'd been taught was that, if they didn't answer the call, something was terribly wrong. In that case, an operative was told to retreat to the nearest safehouse and to keep trying to call.

"I wiped them out. There's no protocol for if the handlers *never* answer again. They're all gone except for the Master."

"Is that really what you think?" Her eyes twinkled in amusement. "I think you skipped a class or two."

She advanced on him again – if he wanted answers, he was going to have to beat them out of her.

Herron was ready this time. He had an advantage in height and weight, but she was fast and aggressive. He wanted to keep her at a distance, where his superior reach gave him an advantage. If they fought in close, he'd lose the edge and it'd be an even contest.

Herron threw a couple of jabs. She fended them off easily but they helped to keep her at a distance. She tried to get inside his guard several times and Herron responded violently. The first time, he tagged her with a left hook. The second, he landed a right jab. He was slowly gaining the upper hand, wearing her down with his superior size and negating her speed advantage by keeping her at arm's length.

Then he aimed a powerful hook right at her head and she dodged it, catching him out of position. Herron didn't get his guard back up in time and grunted when her right elbow hit him in the jaw so hard it sent him to the ground. She was on top of him in a flash, delivering knee after knee to his head. If it was a mixed martial arts fight, she'd have won. Luckily for Herron, real fights don't take place in the octagon.

As the blows pelted down on him, he gripped her throat and bucked his body, moving her weight enough to roll her to the ground and shift on top of her. He had the advantage now. He kept his right hand in a tight grip around her throat, squeezing so hard her focus shifted immediately to defense. She clubbed repeatedly at his hand and arm, but it was no good.

"If you agree to tell me what you know and help me find the Master, you'll live," Herron said. "Otherwise I'll keep squeezing until your eyes pop out of your skull."

She punched, kicked and bucked, but Herron was too strong. The seconds ticked by and she became more desperate, until eventually she stopped fighting and tapped his arm desperately. Herron nodded, let go of her throat slightly and let her take a deep breath. He was ready for her to resume fighting, but she remained compliant. He'd won and he'd have to trust she'd co-operate.

To make sure of it, he socked her as hard as he could on the side of the head.

Herron watched her eyes go glassy as she lost consciousness, and then he climbed off her. He couldn't risk someone so deadly lying about her surrender. He walked over to her pistol, reloaded the magazine and then aimed the weapon at her as she came around. Spitting blood, he was irritated when a tooth went flying with it. He watched it bounce along the road.

Then, as the woman's eyes blinked open, he grinned at her through bloodied lips. "I liked you better when you were tied up."

* * *

Herron parked the car in the motel parking lot. No other

mission he'd ever worked had been as demanding as this one and he wasn't finished yet. But for now, it was time to rest. After the fistfight by the side of the road, he'd stolen a car, bundled the female operative into the trunk and driven until they reached a backwater town. Herron had pulled over at the first motel he'd seen.

As he walked to reception, he could hear his prisoner pounding on the inside of the trunk. He didn't care. His car was the only one in the parking lot and nobody else was around. She was making a whole lot of noise that nobody would hear. Once he reached reception, he waited at the wood-panelled counter until a staff member emerged from the back room.

The woman mumbled something in German, but when it was clear Herron couldn't understand her, she sighed and spoke in English. "Room?"

"Yes." Herron nodded and put a fistful of Euros on the counter.

She scooped up the cash and slammed a set of keys down in its place, neglecting to give him any change. "Check-out is at noon."

Herron took the keys and returned to the car. He drew his pistol, opened the trunk and aimed down at the female operative. "Howdy!"

"You're the worst driver in Europe! I'm going to flay every shred of skin from your body for making me go through that."

Herron ignored her. He was focused on getting her inside the room as fast as he could. "Climb out and head for Room 4. If you do anything else, I'll shoot your ass off."

She pushed herself into a seated position and climbed out of the trunk. "You could have at least helped me out of there."

Herron shrugged, closed the trunk and followed her to the room. Once they were inside, he told her to sit on the sofa and then he moved to the bed. Never taking the pistol off her, he removed the pillowcases from each of the four pillows. She looked at him quizzically when he tossed them at her.

She looked down at them and then back up Herron. "What are these for?"

"Use one to tie your ankles together. Make it tight."

She laughed. "Tying me up worked so well last time."

"This time I'm not relying on idiot bikers to keep you secure."

Herron waited until she'd bound her ankles tight, then ordered her to get onto the floor and sit next to the coffee table. When she was in position, he inched closer and helped her to tie one of her hands to the leg of the heavy oak furnishing. Only then did he put the pistol down – out of her reach – and tie her other hand to the table using the third pillowcase. He stuffed the last one into her mouth.

He picked up the pistol again and looked down at her in triumph. He had a cracking headache, a missing tooth and was walking with a limp – but he'd prevailed. He opened the mini bar and raided it for peanuts, chips, cookies, bottled water and soda. He figured the generous tip he'd left at reception would cover the tab. As he took some time to eat and drink, she looked at him with desperation in her eyes.

Herron put a bottle of water and a few cookies in front of her. "Ready to talk?"

"Mmm!" She nodded.

"If you make any sort of disturbance the gag goes right back in." Herron pulled the gag from her mouth. "Hungry? Thirsty?"

"Yes."

"Okay." Herron fed pieces of cookie to her and then held out the water, which she guzzled down. "Listen. If a handler goes quiet we're taught to retreat to a safehouse. I know that. But I wiped out the handlers and the Master is on the run. There's no one left to call those safehouses. So why do you think there's more to it?"

"You really think the Master fled America because he was afraid of you? That's cute." She gave a small laugh. "He's one of the most powerful men on the planet. He has dozens of elite killers at his disposal. Killing the handlers doesn't change that. He'll just find new ones."

"I'm getting tired of the drip-feed of information. What happens after operatives retreat to a safehouse?"

She shrugged. "If nobody answers for two weeks it means the entire Enclave network is compromised. In that case, we're all to go to the same location and wait for whatever is left of the leadership to arrive.

When they do, the entire structure is rebuilt. New handlers are appointed and assigned operatives."

"Why didn't my handler tell me any of this?" Herron sighed. "It doesn't matter. Tell me where the meeting will occur and I'll take down the Master there."

She smirked. "Even if you kill him, the meeting will go ahead and bring the Enclave back from the dead."

What is dead can rise again. The operative's words at the hospital in Washington hit Herron like a bat to the head.

"It's the Lazarus Protocol," she continued. "It's a shitty name for a plan to resurrect a cabal of assassins, but if you want to stop it, you'll have to set me free."

Herron stared at her with disbelief, but she calmly held his gaze. If she was lying, she was convincing. Besides, what she said made some sense. It explained why the Master had fled to Europe and why she'd just been cooling her heels at the Amsterdam safehouse. There was a good chance the Master was on his way to rebuild the Enclave.

It changed the game. He wasn't chasing the Master anymore, he was trying to prevent the reboot of the entire Enclave.

"Tell me where the meeting will take place."

She shook her head. "Only if you agree to take me too. Decide quickly though – it's happening soon."

Herron considered. If she was right, there was no time to waste arguing. "I agree. Now, where is it?"

"You think I'm stupid?" She laughed. "I'll tell you when we get there."

"Okay."

She paused. "Can I have a gun?"

"You think *I'm* stupid?"

9

HERRON STIFLED a yawn as his car roared past another highway sign informing him he was a few miles closer to London. He wished for the thousandth time that the female operative had told him exactly when and where in the United Kingdom the meeting would take place, but she was keeping that to herself. At least she'd finally told him her name – Frances Charlesworth.

After leaving Germany, they'd driven to the ferry terminal in Calais, France, and crossed the English Channel after completing their passport checks. Once on U.K. soil, he'd stolen another car and they'd settled in for their drive to London. They were now an hour out of Dover and would arrive in London after another hour of uncomfortable silence.

Herron didn't trust Charlesworth and the feeling was probably mutual. He only needed her as a ticket to the meeting and she only needed him to stay alive – it was an alliance of convenience that could end at any moment. He just had to make sure that when that happened, he was the one left standing.

When they were on the outskirts of London, an hour later, Herron turned to her. "What happens when we get to this meeting?"

"One step at a time. We need to get to Trafalgar Square. Then I'll tell you when and where the meeting will take place, and then we'll go our separate ways."

"Unacceptable." Herron frowned. "You said you'd take me to the meeting, not bail right before it."

"The deal has changed. I'll give you the location, but I want no part of what you're doing. You'll be amongst dozens of operatives and the second you're spotted you're a dead man. And if they realize I brought you there, I'll be killed too."

"You don't get that choice." Herron pulled the car over to the side of the road, drew the pistol and aimed it at her. "Stay until I put a bullet in the Master's skull or I put one in yours now."

"You don't get it, do you? Even if you get to the meeting and kill him, what do you think happens next? You kill him, they kill you, the meeting proceeds and a new leadership forms. You're on a suicide mission and I don't want to go down in flames with you."

She was right. Herron had thought all he needed to do to destroy the Enclave was kill its leadership, but only by eradicating the entire Enclave – each and every operative – could he rid the world of its rot. Only its complete annihilation would finish this chapter of his life.

She smiled. "What if I trade you something to let me go...."

"What?"

"We both know you can't do this alone, but I don't want to help you either. I can get you some reinforcements. Better ones than a biker gang, too."

"Who?"

"MI5." She paused to let Herron digest the news. "My last mission for the Enclave was to take down its Director-General. He's been investigating the Enclave's presence in Europe and was getting a little close for my handler's comfort. But when I called my handler for the final green light there was no answer."

"So, you went to ground?"

"Yep."

"And now you somehow think MI5 will help me? That doesn't add up."

"The Director-General's name is Kevin Charlesworth. Yes, my father is the head of a spy agency, but he doesn't know his daughter is an elite assassin who's killed 34 people."

Herron couldn't believe it. He'd cut ties with his own loved ones, but that didn't mean he'd kill them if ordered. "Some family. And he'll help me?"

"For the chance to learn where I am and take

down the Enclave? You bet he will. Look, if I prove he's my father, you'll let me go?"

Herron knew it was time to choose. She was offering to tell him when the meeting was and where it was being held, and dangling the help of MI5 to wipe it out. In return, she wanted simply to walk away. He didn't trust her, but he believed her – he'd reached the end of the line. He was a one-man wrecking ball, able to take down most targets and then disappear afterwards, but he wasn't Superman and this wasn't about one target.

"Okay."

He got them back on the road and resumed the drive. They didn't speak. They'd said everything they needed to. The London traffic was busy, but they arrived without incident and Herron found a spot in a parking garage off Leicester Square. From there it was less than five minutes' walk to Trafalgar Square and the base of Nelson's Column. Without asking Herron for permission, Frances borrowed a phone from a passing college student.

"Let me see what you're doing." Herron didn't want her to do anything that would warn the Enclave. "Prove you're who you say you are and do nothing else."

He needn't have worried. She Googled her father's name and hundreds of photos appeared in the search. She scrolled down for a while, until she found one of her whole family, then turned the screen to show him.

It was her, standing next to the Director-General of MI5.

"Thanks." Herron held the phone out to the guy she'd borrowed it from and waited until the stranger was out of earshot. "Okay, you've convinced me."

"The meeting will be held in Bath at midnight tonight. The Master and all Enclave operatives will be there. Go to MI5, tell my father I sent you and I'm certain he'll help."

"How will he know I'm not lying?"

"Tell him I'm sorry for that last night in Belfast. He'll know then. And he'll do anything you want if you promise it'll lead him back to me."

Herron nodded. Their bargain struck, he waited under Nelson's Column until she'd vanished from sight, thinking all the while how fitting it was that he should be here. Admiral Horatio Nelson was best known for several decisive British naval victories in the Napoleonic Wars – most notably facing terrible odds and prevailing nonetheless. Though his campaign had ultimately cost him his life, his successes had changed the course of history.

Herron hoped Horatio's luck rubbed off on him, minus the dying part.

* * *

Herron paused outside Thames House and stared up at its squat, grey façade. Inside was the headquarters of the British Security Service, MI5 – the government spy agency he was going to ask to take down the Master and the Enclave, likely at the cost of his own liberty. No matter the odds, however, he was glad to have a plan. Now he just had to execute it.

After leaving Trafalgar Square, he'd walked back to the car and driven the short distance to the MI5 headquarters, on the north bank of the River Thames. While MI5 worked to secure Britain from enemies both foreign and domestic, little did they know the bombshell Herron was about to drop on them - it would make all the other threats they were facing seem like a child's game. He just hoped they took him seriously.

"Here goes nothing." He took a deep breath and headed for the entrance.

Herron was a man used to living in the shadows and occasionally striking out to kill. Now he was walking into the light, to confess what he'd started and ask for help to finish it. There was every chance MI5 would simply arrest him and lock him up forever, but he needed to try. He'd sworn to Jessica he'd destroy the Enclave, and to Kearns that he'd keep her safe. This was the only way to live up to both promises.

It was also the key to his own absolution.

He was surprised when nobody moved to intercept him as he got closer to the building. If he strolled up to the CIA's headquarters in Langley or the NSA's headquarters at Fort Meade, he'd expect *some* attention. But the only thing bothering him outside Thames House was the dull, overcast sky. It had always bewildered him that British cops didn't routinely carry firearms – if they did, would he have made it to within spitting distance of their internal security agency without consequence?

But while Herron was usually happy to avoid attention, this time he needed it. He pulled out his pistol, fired a shot into the air and then tossed the weapon onto the ground.

At first nothing happened, then the doors to the building burst open and a half-dozen armed personnel streamed out and rushed to him. They had their weapons drawn – a mix of pistols and submachine guns – and nasty expressions on their faces.

Herron moved his arms out to the side, showing he wasn't a threat. "I'm here to hand myself in. I'm an assassin guilty of over 150 murders. I want to speak to your Director-General."

"Fat chance of that, mate." The head of the security detail said as they all formed a ring around him. "Put your hands on your head, drop to your knees and lay flat on your face."

Herron nodded and complied with their instructions. He knew that one wrong move would end him, so he complied slowly. When he was finally face down on the ground, he heard them move in all around him. They cuffed him, searched him for more weapons and then dragged him to his feet. He smiled at the head of the detail, who dug into his pocket and pulled out a hood.

"I want to speak to your Director-General."

Herron repeated. "I have information about his daughter's disappearance."

"Shut your mouth." The agent lowered the hood over Herron's head. "After the shit you just pulled you'll be lucky to ever see daylight again."

Herron kept quiet as he was shoved in the direction of Thames House. An agent was gripping each of his arms, a sign that they considered him dangerous despite the fact he was cuffed and hooded. He couldn't see anything and there was no sound except for the footfalls of the agents around him. They were well-drilled and efficient.

In less than a minute they were inside the building. The temperature increased significantly and there was a great deal of noise around him. Though his security detail might be silent, the lobby of Thames House had the same low-level buzz of office buildings the world over. He could hear a dozen conversations that paused as he passed, but he didn't catch anything of use.

Even the quiet chatter petered out and died as he was taken deeper into the building and down some stairs. Herron knew he was in the right place when he heard a heavy steel door slam behind them. Though there'd be a thousand people working in Thames House – a mix of agents and bureaucrats – there'd also be a more...private area. It was there MI5 would get many of its answers and solve many of its problems.

Herron was hoping they'd help him solve one of his own.

Finally, they came to a stop. He heard a scraping sound and was struck in the stomach. He grunted and doubled over in pain. Unseen hands forced him to sit in a chair and used cable ties to bind his wrists and ankles to its arms and legs. Only then did the agents holding his arms let go.

He sat in silence and waited. He was working to their timeline now.

He just hoped he'd used enough bait to tempt the big fish to bite.

Sometime later, the hood was pulled from his head without warning. Herron blinked rapidly, helping his eyes adjust to the light and taking in his surroundings. As expected, he was in some sort of basement holding room. The walls and ceiling were concrete, the door solid steel. There was nothing in the room except the chair he was sitting on and a security camera in one corner.

The same agent who'd put the hood on his head had just removed it. He smiled. "Hello, Bambi. Welcome to the home of the original spy catchers. I'm Agent Lever."

Herron shuffled in his chair. "I—"

Lever nodded at someone standing behind Herron. He knew what was coming, but still grunted as pain exploded in the back of his head. He shook off the hit and looked up at Lever with fury in his eyes. He'd come here for help and expected some rough treatment, but he was already getting a little tired of the MI5 man and his crew.

"You don't speak unless spoken to." Lever leaned

in close to Herron's face. "The people working here fucked the Germans, the Soviets and the Islamic terrorists. So, forgive my scepticism when an American comes to our door, fires shots into the air and makes some outlandish claims. Tell me why I should care about you or you'll rot in a concrete box."

Herron smiled inside, but he kept his face neutral. His bait had worked. They were interested in him. Intrigued by him. Now he had to close the deal. He was going to give them his whole life story – a man who'd lived in the shadows and shed dozens of identities – in the hope that these people might give him the help he needed.

"My name is Mitch Herron. I was an American soldier for eight years – regular Army and then the Rangers. Then I was approached to do contract work. I left the military, received more training and then undertook contract killing for an organization called the Enclave. Over eight years, I killed 149 people on their orders."

Herron waited for Lever to say something, but when he kept quiet he continued. "Several months ago, a group of terrorists almost succeeded in unleashing a new strain of weaponized smallpox into the population. I stopped it, but in doing so I disobeyed the Enclave and was cast out."

Lever held up a hand. "Now you're here to ask for our help to get them off your ass? Sorry, not interested."

"No, not quite." Herron took a deep breath. "Turns out my old employers killed the innocent and guilty alike. I've taken down most of their leadership, but one man survived. He's traveled here to meet with whatever remains of his set-up. If that meeting occurs, the organization will reform and more innocents will die. *That's* what I need your help for."

Lever didn't respond. He simply turned and left the room.

* * *

Herron sighed for what felt like the hundredth time. He'd been left alone in the concrete room since his confession to Lever, restrained and helpless until the MI5 agents decided to return. He'd tried shouting for attention but had gone unanswered, so had resigned himself to waiting, even though the Enclave meeting was creeping ever closer.

He found it ironic that he was back in custody less than a week after he'd escaped from the police in Washington D.C. He doubted MI5 were as sloppy as suburban cops, so if they didn't want to work with him he probably wouldn't be able to get away this time. He figured it was the toss of a coin whether they helped him or not. They were just as like to leave him to rot in a cell for the rest of his life.

He lost track of time...as it slipped away, so did his hopes of killing the Master and eradicating the Enclave once and for all. It was like he'd successfully completed most of the race only to stumble on the final hurdle. If he failed, all his work would be for nothing. The Enclave would reform and be back to its evil business within days.

Finally the screech of the heavy steel door heralded the return of his captors. The same crew as before spilled into the room, with Agent Lever standing in front of Herron and his crew taking up position around the edges. A second after they were in position and pointing an array of weapons at him, a new player walked in. Herron recognized him from his picture.

"I'm Kevin Charlesworth." The man crossed the room and stood next to Lever. "You claim to have information about the group I'm targeting and about my daughter."

"You look older than the photo Frances showed me."

"I'm a busy man and you're a criminal." Charlesworth's voice was harsh and he regarded Herron like he might a squashed bug on the sole of his boot. "Get on with it."

"Your daughter Frances sent me." Herron recited the next words carefully, exactly as she'd spoken them. "She said to apologize for that last night in Belfast."

Charlesworth showed no emotion as he kept his eyes locked on Herron. For a few moments, it seemed like Frances had lied, and Herron started to worry. Then cracks appeared in the spymaster's hard-as-nails demeanor. Charlesworth looked down for a moment, and when he looked back to Herron his eyes had a curiosity and a hope that'd been lacking before.

"Tell me who you are and why the fuck you walked through my door." Charlesworth fixed Herron with a hard stare. "And then tell me how you know my daughter."

Herron repeated the same story he'd told Lever. Then he asked the million-dollar question, which would determine whether or not Frances had lied to him. "I believe you've been investigating the Enclave? I need your help to take them down. As for your daughter, I don't know her. Not really. She's an Enclave operative I was dealing with over the last few days and she said you'd help me to take them down. She told me you'd know what her apology about Belfast meant."

"Very much so." Charlesworth spoke softly. He seemed distant now. Thoughtful. "There's not another person on Earth who knows about that night or could even guess at its importance. Assuming everything you've told me checks out, why wouldn't I just prosecute you and continue with investigating this organization myself? They've been on my radar since one of their operatives blew up a vehicle carrying three senior Government ministers."

"Because you need my help to eradicate them." Herron shrugged. "You can take me down, sure. But I'm one man who has killed hundreds and is trying to make amends by taking down a group that's killed thousands. You'll never get another opportunity to hit the Enclave when they're this weak. All I ask is that you let me help you sweep away the whole steaming pit of shit."

Herron watched as Charlesworth considered his words. First, he simply stared into space, as if he was weighing up the decision within the confines of his own mind. Then he turned to Agent Lever and they spoke in whispers. Though Herron couldn't hear what was being said, he could catch the gist of it – Lever was tense and wanted to take Herron down, while Charlesworth saw the bigger picture and perhaps even a chance to find his daughter.

He'll do anything you want if you promise it'll lead him back to me.

Herron chewed over Frances' words again, then put his ace on the table. "Your daughter will be at the gathering of the Enclave. This is your one chance to get her back."

Charlesworth crossed his arms over his chest. "If your story checks out you might have a deal. But if you're wasting my time, you'll spend the rest of your life in here."

Herron nodded. "That's fair. It'll all check out. The meeting is at midnight tonight, so don't spend too much time looking into it. Now tell me, what happened in Belfast?"

"That's a family matter. A *classified* family matter."

Charlesworth nodded at Lever and then led the MI5 crew out of the room. Within a few seconds, the door had slammed shut and Herron was alone again. If Charlesworth had been investigating the Enclave and his daughter was an operative, it really was ridiculous that Herron was sitting in the bowels of MI5 trying to convince him to act against them.

This time, the wait was a little shorter. After about an hour, the door squealed open again and Lever entered the room. Herron kept quiet and stood next to the door with a pistol held by his side. Only a few seconds later Charlesworth appeared and walked right over to Herron. Any hint of softness from the earlier mention of his daughter had disappeared and he was the cold spymaster again.

"Your story checks out." Charlesworth paused. "Now I have some very simple questions."

Herron nodded. He knew this was it. "Okay."

"Can you tell me when and where this meeting will take place?"

"Queens Square in Bath. Midnight."

"And will my daughter be there?"

"I think so."

"And you're committed to helping us take down the Enclave?"

"That's the whole reason I'm here."

Charlesworth smiled. "And will you work for MI5 when the Enclave is destroyed?"

Herron hesitated. He'd come so far on the promise of killing the Master, destroying the Enclave and freeing himself and the world of their pestilence. To do so, he was making a deal with the devil, who was offering to amplify his vengeance in return for his freedom. It was a bargain Herron would never have accepted before, but circumstances had changed. People he cared for had died or were still in danger and there was blood on his hands.

The blood of innocents.

Herron nodded. "Once the Master and the Enclave are gone, you can do what you like with me."

Charlesworth smiled like a hyena.

10

HERRON REMAINED silent as he rode the elevator up from the basement of Thames House. Agent Lever and another agent – introduced as Bains – were watching his every move, but despite the escort, he was glad to be free of his restraints. After he'd agreed to Charlesworth's terms, the spymaster had freed him and then immediately disappeared. Herron had been asked more questions by Lever and Bains, then escorted upstairs.

The elevator stopped on the fifth floor, a chime sounding as the doors slid open. He was somewhere special now – the inner sanctum of the British Government's premier domestic security agency.

"Let's go, buddy." Lever placed a hand on his back and gave him a gentle shove. "The Director-General is waiting."

Herron walked down the hallway, with Lever leading the way and Bains behind him. On either side of him were countless offices, each with their door closed and some clandestine business of state going on behind it. He hoped at least some of the brightest brains in the building were figuring out how to disrupt the Enclave meeting, or else the support of MI5 would mean nothing.

"Through here." Lever directed Herron into a large conference room, dominated by a table laid out with plates of pastries and fruit. He pointed to a chair. "Sit."

Herron did so. Lever sat to his left, while Bains remained standing directly behind him. Herron had no doubt he'd eat a bullet if he tried to stand. Though Charlesworth had accepted his bargain, it was clear he had ordered his men to remain vigilant. While he waited, Herron helped himself to the catering. He poured a big glass of water and filled a small plate with muffins.

Herron made it most of the way through a plate of food before a group of people in suits walked in. Charlesworth and his small entourage arrived last, taking up positions at the head of the table. When everyone was seated, Herron guessed there were around twenty people around the table. Given he was used to working alone, it seemed like an army had gathered to take down the Enclave.

Charlesworth cleared his throat and the buzz of conversation died down. "Thanks for making time everyone. This is big."

Herron sat back, watching as Charlesworth brought them up to speed. He felt their eyes on him when their boss revealed his part in all this, but the looks were fleeting. All attention was on Charlesworth as he explained the opportunity to wipe out a cell of the worst killers – the worst terrorists – on the planet when they were at their weakest.

"Andrea Bricknell will explain the detail." Charlesworth gestured with his chin towards a woman sitting a few seats down the table to his left. "She's worked this one up."

Herron watched Bricknell as she nodded at Charlesworth and took over the briefing. She was about forty, and oozed competence and confidence. She'd clearly risen to the highest levels in a male-dominated environment and obviously had the respect of her colleagues. She pointed a remote at the wall and pressed a button. The lights dimmed and a map was projected onto the space.

"This is Queen's Square in Bath, where Mr Herron tells us the meeting will take place at midnight tonight." She clicked and four arrows appeared – one at each entrance to the square. "The strategic situation is complex, because through a terrible quirk of timing, a local Jane Austen festival will mean vastly more civilians than usual are on the street tonight."

One of the executives leaned forward. "Could we cancel the festival?"

Bricknell shook her head. "No, it would be a dead giveaway and they'd likely disperse and cost us our chance. We'll just have to manage the situation. So, when the meeting begins, four tactical teams will converge on the space. We'll have one backup team on the ground, another team in the air, snipers on the rooftops and drones on station. If all—"

Herron interrupted Bricknell. "This all sounds a little pedestrian. This is a group of the best killers on the planet. You need to hit them way harder than that."

Charlesworth held up a hand to forestall Bricknell's response and threw an icy glare at Herron. "You may think you have a say, Mr Herron, but make no mistake about your role here. You'll be in Bath to eyeball the Master and confirm his presence. After that moment, your role is done. Any other views you have are irrelevant to me. This is our operation."

Herron nodded. There was nothing to say. The balance of power here was clear. He sat back and crossed his arms.

Charlesworth lapsed into silence while Bricknell finished outlining the operation, then he looked around the table. "If everyone is satisfied, I'll call the Prime Minister."

He picked up his cell phone and dialled. The call was answered quickly and the spymaster kept his features neutral, his voice low and his hand covering his mouth as he spoke. As the seconds ticked by, there was an electricity in the room. Herron knew the feeling well. It was the collective buzz of an upcoming mission – equal parts excitement and fear – which would reach a violent crescendo.

After several minutes, Charlesworth terminated

the call and turned back to the conference room. The conversation up and down the table quickly died down and every MI5 staffer turned their eyes to their boss. Herron already knew what Charlesworth was going to say, because there was only one thing for him *to* say. No national leader would let a group of elite assassins hold a meeting on their soil without trying to stop it.

Charlesworth's look was ashen. "We have authorization. We commence in one hour."

Herron stayed put as the twenty or so MI5 staff rose from their seats and hurried out to prepare. Only Charlesworth, Bains and Lever remained, the two agents staying on guard duty while their boss sat down directly opposite Herron.

Charlesworth locked Herron with an icy glare. "Just to be absolutely unambiguous: Agents Lever and Bains will ensure you do precisely what you're told and nothing else. They have orders to execute you at the first sign of trouble. You stay with Lever and Bains; you confirm the Master's identity; and you keep quiet when the fireworks start. Clear?"

Herron nodded. "Crystal."

* * *

"Now arriving in Bath." Lever smiled at Herron from the seat opposite him. "You might never leave."

Herron rolled his eyes at Lever's dripping sarcasm. The MI5 agent had a smile on his face and a pistol in his lap, and had been needling Herron for the entire van ride from London to the ancient town. He hadn't risen to the bait – he had no doubt Lever and Bains would take him out without hesitation if needed, so there was no point responding to the barbs.

His only objective was to bring the hammer of MI5 down on the Enclave.

At Thames House, he'd been bundled into the back of a black van long before the MI5 crews had mounted up, Lever and Bains keeping him company the whole time. They'd traveled in a 12-vehicle convoy; Herron wasn't sure how many Enclave operatives there would be to deal with, but he hoped the agency had packed enough heat. They had only a few hours to prepare before the meeting was due to commence.

He returned to looking out the window, just in time to see four black SUVs peel off from the convoy and take a right turn. The move replicated one another group of vehicles had taken five minutes earlier, splitting off to take up their position prior to the operation. About half the transports were driving into the town itself, including the van Herron was riding in. Ahead of his vehicle all he could see was a precession of red tail lights.

Only a few minutes later, the remaining vehicles slowed to a stop. Agents bundled out, secured the street, then moved out in small groups with their weapons and gear. Lever and Bains didn't move an inch while this was all happening, staying seated in the back of the van with their eyes locked onto Herron. Only when the last of the MI5 agents had disappeared from sight did his escorts make a move.

"If you do anything except what you're told, we'll put you down." Lever raised an eyebrow at Herron. "You know the rules."

"Don't unleash my mad superhero skills and always floss when I brush." Herron scoffed. "You guys really are paranoid. I came to you, remember?"

Lever didn't respond. Instead, he climbed out of the van and looked around. The convoy had stopped in front of a row of unremarkable homes, lit only by the pale moonlight and the street lights. But when the agents motioned for him to enter one of the townhouses, it was clear to Herron that there was more going on inside than residential bliss.

It had to be some sort of MI5 facility.

Bains gripped one of Herron's arms and led him straight inside. The interior didn't have the usual trappings of a private residence – there were few internal walls and none of the normal furniture. Instead, there was a giant conference table with a number of computer terminals atop.

He stood in the corner of the room, Lever and Bains watching him like a hawk. Other MI5 agents were rushing around urgently, removing protective sheets from the terminals and booting up the computers. There was an organized efficiency to the agents that was impressive. Each executed their role perfectly. It was like watching a military unit in action.

"We're not quite like the FBI, Mr Herron," Charlesworth said as he entered the room. "We're better."

Herron shrugged. "I hope so, because they never dealt with the Enclave on American soil. We'll see if you guys are up to it."

"We'll have access to every security-camera feed in the city, as well as the portable feeds my agents and aerial drones will be streaming to this headquarters. We've got enough eyes and guns on the square to contain the meeting. Once you confirm the Master's identity, we'll move in and smash them to pieces."

Herron doubted it would go as smoothly as that, but he couldn't fault the plan and he kept his doubts to himself. "Sounds fine."

"This would be easier if you told us what the Master looked like." Charlesworth fixed Herron with a hard stare. "We could find him in seconds."

"Then you wouldn't need me for anything..."

Herron's voice trailed off and Charlesworth gave up on trying to force a description out of him. MI5 hadn't figured out the link between Herron and the attack on the hospital back in the States, so they hadn't tracked down the news report of the incident or the video of the Master that went with it. Herron was happy for their help, but he needed to stay useful to them. He didn't want them freezing him out of the operation entirely.

A few minutes later, the command center was up and running. Agents were sitting at computer terminals and camera feeds were projecting onto the screen at the head of the table. Though it would have been easier to spot the Master in the daylight, the feeds were good enough to do the job. One feed dominated – the view of Queen's Square, where the meeting was taking place – while other views cycled through at the edges of the screen.

"Sit and watch," Charlesworth ordered.

Herron was escorted to one of the seats at the table. As soon as he was seated, he started to scan the camera feeds, searching for a sign of the Master while also keeping his eye on the main view of the square. Though the assassins and their leader would be alert for any danger, there was no way they'd know how much attention the authorities were currently paying to the historic town of Bath.

Seconds and minutes ticked by, until almost an hour had been wasted with no sign of the Master. Though Herron had hoped the square would empty out as midnight drew closer, the Jane Austen festival was keeping people out later than usual. Civilians loitered around in small groups – were some of them Enclave operatives? The key to unlocking the meeting and identifying all the enemy agents was finding the Master. Herron's eyes were darting around the screens, taking in every face from every camera, trying to locate his prey.

Charlesworth was growing impatient. "If you're stringing us along, you're going to spend a very long time inside a very dark hole, Mr Herron."

Herron simply pointed at the screen. "There he is. I suggest you start tracking his every move."

Charlesworth pounded the table with a fist. "You're sure?"

"I'm sure." The man on the screen was unmistakable. It was the same man who'd tricked him at the hospital. It was the Master.

Charlesworth began barking orders at his subordinates. "Task a drone to track him wherever he goes. I want to know if he so much as scratches his head. Get the tactical teams close to the square ready to strike. But nobody moves on him unless I give the order. Clear?"

The MI5 agents sprang into action. It wouldn't be by his own hand, but Herron's triumph was close.

A drone flying high up in the sky over Bath turned its camera to the Master and the tactical teams converged on Queen's Square from every direction. They were represented on the digital map of the city by little dots, one for each agent. A team of six was moving on each entrance to the square and there were shooters on the rooftops.

"We've got them." Charlesworth smiled as the Master entered the square. "Tactical teams prepare to move in. Be aware of high civilian traffic in the area. Primary target is an older male wearing jeans, a red sweater, and a black cap. Bag him if you can. Secondary targets are unknown, but assumed. Lethal force authorized on anyone who is armed."

As commanders implemented Charlesworth's orders and issued a few of their own, Herron squinted at the video screen. Something wasn't right.

One of the smaller feeds being relayed from a drone had caught his attention.

Herron turned to the agent operating the screen and deciding which angles to show. "Can you maximize feed four so it's larger on the screen?"

"Sure." The agent started to do as he'd been asked, then looked to Bains and Lever for permission. They nodded, and a second later the display changed to show the feed.

Herron's eyes widened. The niggling unease in the back of his mind now howled like a klaxon.

A group of five or so people stood in the middle of the square and each entrance to the square had two groups of three people standing on either side of it. Despite the festival, the pattern and the distribution of numbers was too perfect. What looked like random clusters of civilians were almost certainly not. Nobody on the ground would notice, but the drone feed showed it clearly.

Herron saw it clearly.

It was a trap.

"Looks like the Master is headed for the group in the middle of the square." Charlesworth grinned and barked the order before Herron could stop him. "Execute!"

* * *

Herron turned to Charlesworth. "You need to abort. They know you're coming! They have all along!"

"You need to be quiet." Charlesworth's glare was icy. "We've got them. It's all over except the fireworks."

"You don't understand!" Herron tried to get to his feet, but Bains and Lever forced him back down. "Bricknell's tactical teams are about to get shredded!"

Charlesworth turned to watch the camera as the tactical teams surged into the square, moving with perfect timing. They had been told to make straight for the group standing in the middle of the square, and moved with confidence and purpose, twenty-four heavily armed agents quickly surrounding the group.

There was no shooting. The cluster of Enclave agents had been caught cold. For a moment, Herron thought he might be wrong. Then the screens lit up with the flashes of gunfire and panicked reports started coming in over the radio.

"Alpha team under fire!"

"Getting shot at from behind!"

"Charlie taking casualties!"

"All teams under fire, sir!"

"Delta Prime is down!"

Herron, Charlesworth and the other MI5 agents in the command center saw the situation play out from above. After their teams had moved deeper into the square, the Enclave operatives near the entrances had started to fire into their backs. As soon as the MI5 agents had turned to face the new threat, the Enclave group in the center – including the Master – had drawn their weapons and added to the Brits' problems.

It was a classic envelopment and ambush of an overconfident foe. Herron had used the same tactics in the special forces, now he was watching a perfect example of its application. Though the MI5 sharpshooters on the rooftops were doing their best to support their ground teams, numbers favored the Enclave. For every Enclave operative that dropped, two MI5 agents went down. The battle was going to shit.

Herron watched the slaughter with a strange detachment, even though he knew men and women were dying down there. His best chance to kill the Master and beat the Enclave was slipping away. Charlesworth and the others were also staring at the screens, too stunned by the situation to react.

"Pull them out!" Herron's shout broke their trance. "Order them to pull back to one exit. Cover them with your shooters and send your backup teams to help."

Charlesworth blinked a few times, stared at Herron and then nodded. "All teams withdraw from the square using the south-east exit. Staged withdrawal, each team covering the next in turn. Rooftop shooters have full clearance. Scramble the backup teams to the south-east exit."

As his subordinates relayed the orders, Herron caught Charlesworth's eye. He was glad the Director-General's head was back in the game. Though the chance to take down the Enclave was probably blown, some of the MI5 agents might escape the ambush and live. It was the only victory that could possibly be won today, unless someone got lucky and took down the Master amidst the chaos.

"Sir..." One of the surveillance controllers spoke with a shaky voice. "They're retreating as well."

Herron and Charlesworth both looked at the screen. As the MI5 team moved to the south-east exit from the square, the Master and a core group of Enclave operatives was moving to the north-west. The two groups were still exchanging fire and shooters on both sides were still dropping, but the distance between them was growing and the gunfire was slackening. It was another surprise in a situation full of them.

"We can still get the Master." Herron tried to stand again, but he was once again pushed down by Bains and Lever. "Let me go after him!"

Lever drew his pistol and pressed it into Herron's skull. "You were told to sit in that chair. I won't tell you again."

Charlesworth shook his head. "Herron's right. We're never going to get this chance again. Once they disperse, we lose our shot to take them down. Gear up."

One of Charlesworth's subordinates shook her head. "Sir, we don't have the numbers to go after them. The backup teams are committed. We need to let this one go."

"We have the numbers." Charlesworth looked around the room and drew his pistol. "Agent Lever, stay with Herron. Agent Daniels, maintain operational oversight and tell Agent Bricknell to rally her teams in the square and get ready to move once I arrive. Everyone else, on me."

Herron tried to protest his exclusion, but Lever only pressed the pistol harder into his skull. Except for Lever and Daniels – the agent told to stay in command of the whole shit show – everyone in the operations center produced weapons and filed out after Charlesworth. Within a few seconds, the headquarters went from bustling to still.

Herron sat in tense silence, unable to push the issue while he had a gun against his head. A few seconds after the house had cleared out, however, Lever lowered the pistol and resumed his overwatch position. Clearly he thought Herron would stop protesting now the rest of the agents had set off to hunt the Master.

He was wrong.

Herron planted his feet and pushed himself up from the chair. In one explosive motion he brought the crown of his skull up into Lever's chin. The sound was sickening, and Lever's surprised grunt told him all he needed to know. As Herron stood to his full height and turned around, Lever stumbled back, one hand to his face. There was every chance his jaw was broken and the pain must have been considerable.

"Give me the gun." Herron held out his hand. "I don't want to hurt you unless you force me to."

Lever consider his options for a split second, then started to raise the pistol. Herron gripped his wrist and twisted it inward until it broke. As Lever cried out in pain, Herron wrapped his other hand around the pistol barrel and pulled. Lever couldn't maintain his grip with the broken wrist, and within a second Herron was armed once more.

He took a step back, pointing the weapon at the agent. Neither Lever nor Daniels resisted any further. Lever was too badly hurt; Daniels was too busy coordinating MI5 assets to care about the scuffle. He simply shrugged his shoulders, turned away from Herron and went back to relaying information to the tactical teams. He was smart.

Herron kept the pistol trained on Lever as he reached down to grab an earpiece from the table. "Wait here. I'm going to kill the Master and save your colleagues."

11

HERRON BURST out of the townhouse and ran towards the square. It was only a few blocks away but he had to fight through the stream of civilians who were headed in the opposite direction. A minute ago they'd been enjoying a festival, now they were frightened by the chaos and the gunfire. He just had to hope the foot traffic was slowing down the Master's escape as well. Police sirens wailed, but the gunfire had stopped for now.

He was furious at himself for not spotting the ambush earlier. But the only way the Enclave could have known MI5 was coming for them was if Frances Charlesworth had warned them. There was no other explanation. He'd spared her life and she'd sold him out.

With his pistol in one hand, Herron used the other to put in the earpiece he'd picked up. Immediately he could hear updates: Charlesworth and Bricknell barking orders; and updates from the remains of the tactical teams, the sharpshooters, the drone operators and the agent in the command center. It was a mixed situation. The tactical teams had withdrawn and taken up defensive positions, the sharpshooters were out of targets, and the drones were tracking the Master and the few other operatives who'd fled.

It only took a few minutes to arrive in the square, where he found chaos. There were bodies everywhere – MI5 and Enclave alike – and the emergency services were pouring into the area in huge numbers as festivalgoers continued to pour out of the area. Only a few civilians remained – most had bailed at the first sign of gunfire – and it was likely those that still remained in the square had been too scared or too incapable to run when the action started.

In the middle of it all was Charlesworth and Andrea Bricknell, his tactical team leader.

Herron stopped and watched as the MI5 Director-General waved his hands, motioning police to bottle up the scene and paramedics to sort out his wounded. The main game, however, was making sure the wounded Enclave operatives were secured. Herron knew from the feed in his earpiece that Charlesworth had already sent assets after the Master, but he was surprised the Director-General wasn't chasing their foe himself.

Herron strode over to Charlesworth, but the second Bricknell spotted him she raised her submachine gun. Herron held his hands wide. "I'm on your side."

She snarled, the barrel of the gun not wavering at all. "I've got a dozen dead men and women who'd say otherwise if they could. Don't come any closer."

"It's fine, Andrea." Charlesworth walked past her and came closer to Herron. "What the hell are you doing here? And where is Agent Lever?"

"He's fine, but he'll have a headache for a few days." Herron looked around. "The Master is getting away. Give me a few agents and let me go after him."

"Not a chance. I'll be in enough shit after today. I don't want to end up in the official report as the guy who gave a criminal command of MI5 assets. I've sent assets after him."

"It won't be enough." Herron gripped his pistol tighter. "You can do whatever you like, but I'm going after—"

"SHOOTER!" Andrea Bricknell's voice was piercing. "SOUTH EAST BUILDING, THIRD WINDOW!

Herron instinctively crash-tackled Charlesworth to the ground as gunfire and shouts once again filled the square. Herron and the Director-General landed in a tangle of limbs, but it only took a second for Herron to rise again on one knee with his pistol raised. He glanced down at Charlesworth. It didn't look like he'd been hit. Bricknell's warning had probably saved his life.

That was more than could be said for her. She was missing a chunk of her skull.

Herron turned his attention to finding the shooter, starting with the window Bricknell had called out. A fusillade of return fire by the remaining agents had shattered the glass and pockmarked the bricks around the window, but the shooter was already gone. They'd taken the shot and then got the hell out of Dodge. In a few seconds the gunfire died down and the shouts quietened, though every law enforcement officer in the square remained on alert.

Herron climbed to his feet and held out a hand to help Charlesworth. "You need to send assets after the shooter. And the Master."

"Okay." Charlesworth took the hand, climbed to his feet and locked eyes on Bricknell's body. He sighed and looked around at his people. "Did anyone see the shooter?"

"I did." Agent Bains took a step closer, his eyes still scanning for the threat. "Female, red hair. Bricknell called the location right, but the shooter fired and withdrew."

"Frances." The Director-General looked more stunned now than when the ambush had kicked off. "You saved me... my daughter... she missed... I—"

It was as if Charlesworth was in a trance, so shocked by what had happened that he was unable to move or act. Herron couldn't blame him. In the space of two days, the spymaster had found out first that his daughter was alive and then that she was trying to kill him. But there was no time for Charlesworth's internal emotional crisis. People were dying and the Master was getting further away.

Herron squared up to Charlesworth and clamped a hand down on his shoulder. "Time for answers. What happened in Belfast?"

Charlesworth blinked rapidly. "Belfast? I...It's complicated...I didn't want any of that to happen."

"Any of *what*?" Herron shoved him in the chest, causing him to stumble back a step. "Why did your daughter lie to me, lure us into an ambush and then try to kill you?"

"I...Frances joined MI5 straight out of college. She was a brilliant agent and I handled her missions directly."

"Isn't that against some sort of rule?" Herron didn't think it was likely MI5 would approve a father-and-daughter combo.

"I make the rules," Charlesworth snapped. "I got her through fourteen operations unscathed. Then I was ordered to extract our highest-value asset from Belfast. This guy had been on the front line of our work against the IRA for twenty-five years but he'd been found out. Losing him would have been disastrous. He had a lifetime of secrets. Frances was tasked with getting him out. It went south. Frances and the asset were cornered..."

"You burned her, didn't you? You chose your career and the life of an old man over the life of your daughter." Herron shook his head slowly. "You're a piece of shit."

Charlesworth squeezed his eyes shut. "I regret it every single day and I've re-enacted the situation in my head a million times. I'd change it if I could."

"Maybe you can." Herron put a hand on his shoulder and waited for him to open his eyes. "You're a good man who made a bad choice. The Enclave made me do that, too. But now you have the opportunity to make a good one. If you help me take down the Master, we might be able to tell your daughter how you feel as well."

Charlesworth considered Herron's words for a second and then nodded. "I don't have many assets left to spare. It'll be you, me, a few others and some drone coverage."

Herron reached down to grab a submachine gun from a downed tactical agent. "That's all we need."

* * *

Herron dragooned two agents to help track down the Master. He led them and Charlesworth away from the square, where Bains stayed to mop up. They followed the directions of the drone operator who was broadcasting the location of the Master, and who informed them they were slowly gaining on him. By now the civilians had mostly cleared the streets, as news of the gunfire and the slaughter in the square reached them.

Herron turned to Charlesworth, who was jogging next to him. "They seem to be slowing down."

"Maybe he's wounded." Charlesworth's breathing was ragged – he lacked the fitness of Herron and the MI5 agents.

"Possibly. But he's played us so well this whole time that I wouldn't guarantee that this isn't some larger play. I—"

The drone operator spoke in their earpieces, cutting him off. "*Sir, the primary target has entered a house with two others. We've got agents on containment.*"

"Got him." Charlesworth smiled. "Keep those agents outside until we get there. Nobody gets in or out of that building."

Herron frowned. It all seemed too easy. They were only a street away from the house by now. As he flicked off the safety on his submachine gun, the rest of his posse did the same. From up ahead came the chattering of submachine guns and the deeper boom of a rifle.

Herron cursed. "Charlesworth, check in."

Charlesworth nodded and linked comms with the drone controller. There was no fear or hesitation in the spymaster's eyes, despite all that'd gone wrong – Charlesworth wanted to find his daughter as much as Herron wanted to find the Master, though for different reasons.

"*The agents at the front of the house are under attack.*" The voice of the operator was calm, despite the situation. "*Take your next left and then the next right.*"

Herron broke into a run again, the others right behind him. He turned the last corner and pulled up short. Three MI5 agents were sprawled on the ground outside a normal-looking home, all with gunshot wounds: two of them were on their backs, unmoving, while the third was on his side and slowly crawling away from the house.

"Cover me." Herron ran over to the wounded man and knelt beside him. "We'll get some paramedics here to help you."

"Okay." The agent rolled onto his back. He'd been shot in the shoulder and had left a trail of blood as he crawled away. "Who are you?"

"A friend." Herron pressed down on the man's wound to staunch the bleeding. "What happened here?"

The agent coughed. "We had them bottled up from the front and there was another team watching from the back. A woman hit us in the rear and then ran inside."

"A woman?" Charlesworth said. "Did she say anything? Did she look about mid-thirties?"

"Something like that." The agent coughed again. "We were too busy getting our asses handed to us to take a description."

Keeping his submachine gun at the ready, Herron ordered Charlesworth to call in some paramedics. Then he told one of the other agents to check the two fallen men were beyond help, and tasked the other with keeping pressure on the wounded man's shoulder.

His earpiece crackled. "*Director-General, the team at the rear of the building is still intact. The targets are still inside. We have agents converging on your location.*"

"We're not waiting," Charlesworth said. "All the answers are inside."

Herron nodded. "Let's go get them."

He advanced with his submachine gun leveled, taking up position on the left of the door with Charlesworth stacked behind him. One of the agents stood on the opposite side of the entrance.

Herron whispered. "On three."

He nodded once, twice, three times. As the agent pressed down on the handle and eased the door open, gunfire roared from inside the house. Shots ripped through the wooden door, the agent taking the brunt of the fire. He screamed and fell to the ground. Herron cursed and pushed Charlesworth back, out of the line of fire.

"There's no way we can push inside through the door." Charlesworth said through gritted teeth. "It's a suicide mission."

Herron thought a moment. "Can you get in touch with your drone operator one last time?"

"My drone operator? Why? I..." Charlesworth's look of confusion changed into a smile. "Oh, this is going to be fun."

Herron nodded and Charlesworth called in the instructions. Herron still found it strange that the Master and his people had holed up inside a building, but he'd given up trying to figure out the way the man thought. The Master had outsmarted him several times, now Herron was going to outmuscle him.

"*You want me to do what?*" The drone operator sounded shocked. "*Are you sure, sir?*"

"Stop wasting time." Charlesworth said. "Get it

done or I'll find someone who will do what I ask and you'll be manning a desk in the Orkney Islands!"

The abuse worked. There was nothing but silence for thirty seconds then Herron heard a high-pitched whine gradually becoming louder. He took a few more steps back from the door and waited. A moment later, he spotted a small drone descending rapidly and heading straight toward the front door of the house at high speed.

Herron looked back at Charlesworth. "Ready?"

The drone slammed through the front door and crashed inside. The flash of an explosion brightened the night, followed by a muffled boom and cries of pain – their impromptu battering ram had worked.

Herron rounded the door, stepped through it and searched for a target. He assessed the situation in a split-second. The crashing drone had taken down one Enclave operative while another was standing at the top of the stairs. Herron fired first and red blossoms appeared on the woman's chest. She dropped, her own shots going wild.

Herron turned to Charlesworth. "Cover the stairs. If you see anyone – even Frances – you take them down."

He kept moving through the interior, searching each room. He was definitely outnumbered and probably outgunned, but he wouldn't slow down now he was so close. He owed it to Jessica and Erica Kearns and all the innocents he'd killed while in the employ of the Enclave to finish this or die trying.

The front two rooms off the hallway – both

bedrooms – were clear, and so too was the living room at the back of the house.

"Frances!"

Herron cursed as he heard Charlesworth's cry from back near the stairs. He gripped his submachine gun tight and ran towards the shout, hoping the Director-General had the steel to do what was necessary but fearing that he didn't. He reached the stairs and saw Frances at the top, aiming her assault rifle down at her father. He was prepared to fire when Charlesworth stepped in the way.

Herron cursed. "Move!"

"No!" Charlesworth shook his head. "I'm not going to let you hurt her."

* * *

"How sweet of you, father. Shame you didn't show such concern for my wellbeing in Belfast." Frances shifted her aim to Herron. "Drop the weapon."

Herron could have tried to take a shot, right through Charlesworth, but Frances' assault rifle would cut both him and Charlesworth down in a second. The only thing he was concerned about was getting a shot at the Master and dying wouldn't help with that. His best chance was playing along with her. He tossed his submachine gun on the ground and held his hands wide, looking up at Frances and waiting for whatever came next.

"On your knees, both of you." She took a step

down the stairs. "Then lock your hands behind your heads."

Herron and Charlesworth followed her instructions – given Frances had them well covered, Herron was happy to roll with the punches until he got the chance to turn the tables. He looked at the MI5 Director-General, who was finally reunited with the daughter he'd thought dead.

"Frances..." Charlesworth's hard demeanor from a few hours earlier had melted away. Now he resembled an old man, traumatized in the face of his mistakes. "I..."

Frances reached the bottom of the stairs. "You've got a death wish. You should be a corpse right now."

Charlesworth's face was clouded with emotion and he choked back tears. "Frances. Please, you must understand, I—"

"Quiet!" She hit him on the side of the head with the butt of the rifle, sending him sprawling. "Nothing you can say means anything to me. I—"

With the assault rifle pointed away from both him and Charlesworth, Herron moved. With explosive force, he propelled himself up to his feet and forward in one motion. Frances turned, her eyes widening; she realized her mistake a split-second before Herron crash-tackled her to the ground. Her assault rifle clattered to the ground.

It was the second time he'd had her in this position, but she'd learned from their last encounter.

As Herron climbed on top of her and tried to restrain her, she produced a blade, stabbing out at him repeatedly. She'd cut his arm before he could press down on the inside of her elbow and prevent her stabbing him in the stomach or chest. Crying out in pain, he grabbed her wrist with his free hand, twisting until she let go of the knife.

Herron pinned her arms, using his superior strength to subdue her. "You betrayed me."

She struggled to get free, but without the knife she'd lost her advantage. "You were a means to an end."

Herron maneuvered a knee to cover one of her arms. With the hand that freed up, he picked up the knife and put it to her throat. "I was *what*?"

"Don't move an inch!"

The voice boomed through the house, cutting off Frances before she could reply. Herron kept the blade pressed against her throat as he looked for the new arrival.

The Master was slowly descending the stairs, a pistol aimed down at them. He was walking with a limp and a red strain had darkened his chinos near the calf. While that explained how they'd had been able to catch up with him, it didn't matter. He still had the drop on Herron and Charlesworth.

Though Herron doubted talking would do much good, he had to try. "Why come to this place? You've got no chance of escaping."

"Well, this wasn't exactly how I'd envisaged my plan playing out." The Master sighed. "Frances saw to that. But every cloud has a silver lining. If I'd simply fled I'd have been an easy target, but now I've got the

Director-General of MI5 in my grasp. The British won't make a move on me while I have Charlesworth."

"That's your plan?" Herron raised an eyebrow. "It'll fail as badly as your attempt to reform the Enclave."

"Reform the Enclave?" He laughed. "Idiot! I'm the Master until I stop breathing! Though you wiped out the handlers, I still had the contact details for every operative around the world. The Lazarus Protocol is a sham. When it was clear you weren't going to give up chasing me, I put a plan in place to stop you.

"You'd proven to be resourceful and damaging, but you're also predictable. I knew you'd find out I'd fled to Europe and start by looking in the safehouses, so I planted Frances at one of them to feed you bait and lead you here to me. Then I called every agent here to ambush you when you arrived.

The Master gave a bitter laugh. "Unfortunately, Miss Charlesworth went a mile off mission and involved MI5 so she could get her own back on Daddy. I planned to down you using overwhelming force, not lose most of my operatives when half of MI5 showed up to take me down."

"No plan survives contact with the enemy." Herron laughed. His voice was calm, but the Master's words had been like punches in the gut. For weeks he'd chased his target halfway across the world, and all the time he was being maneuvered, led around by the nose into a trap. "It's over. This building is surrounded and MI5 won't let you out of it."

"Forget MI5. I have their Director-General, they won't move on me. Besides, I suspect you wouldn't let them anyway. You see, you're my plan B. I'm wounded and need your help to escape. Your instincts are to kill me, but even you can see you'd be wasting an opportunity. I—"

"No!" Frances cried out. "We're not making a deal with *them*. Shoot him and then shoot my father! It's the only way we win!"

"*We?*" The Master snarled at her. "You've cost me a dozen of my operatives. We planned and deployed to deal with *one man*, not an entire army!"

She flushed red. "I—"

The Master's voice boomed. "MI5 only came here at all because you took it on yourself to freelance, to get revenge on your father!"

Her faced twisted into a grimace. "He left me to die in Belfast! The—"

The Master's pistol boomed and Frances' head jerked. The bullet had hit her between the eyes.

Herron cursed and jerked upright.

"Uh-uh." The Master swung his pistol towards him, gestured for him to drop his weapon. Herron tossed the blade to the ground and held his hands wide.

"Now, as I was trying to say, I'm wounded and I need your help to escape. All we need to do is hold Charlesworth hostage until we're clear." The Master reached the bottom of the stairs, grimacing each time the weight shifted onto his wounded leg. "Ally yourself with me and all is forgiven. You can return to the fold and we'll run the Enclave together."

Herron laughed. "I've dedicated my life to destroy you. People have *died* to destroy you. Why would I stop now?"

"Because I've got an operative watching Erica Kearns. If I don't answer when he calls me every four hours, he kills her. If you kill me, she dies too."

Herron's head swam. A large reason he'd fought so hard to kill the Master and eradicate the Enclave was to keep Kearns safe. Could he accept the Master's terms and turn his back on everything he'd fought for? Could he reject the Master's terms and risk Kearns' death?

It was an impossible choice. But it was one he had to make.

"If I join you, the Enclave stops harming innocents and focuses only on rooting out evil." Herron paused, struggling with the words. "And Kearns is kept safe."

"You'll have a full veto over any mission," the Master said. "And your friend will be safe so long as I can continue to rely on your co-operation."

Herron nodded. He looked down at Frances Charlesworth's body, feeling a momentary pang of sadness for her. She'd been betrayed by her father and then by her Master. She'd paid the ultimate price. For his part, Director-General Charlesworth was still sprawled out on the ground, but he was starting to come around.

"I have a boat waiting for us. It's powerful enough

to get us across the Channel and back to Europe." The Master gestured at Charlesworth with his pistol. "Once he's back on his feet, we'll take him as a hostage and head for the boat. If there's any trouble, you might need to shoot our way out of here."

"I can do that. Just make sure no harm comes to Kearns."

Herron reached down and grabbed Frances' assault rifle. Slowly, Charlesworth regained consciousness. He blinked and looked up at the Master, who smirked down at his prisoner. The head of the Enclave said something to Charlesworth – gloating – but Herron wasn't listening. He'd made his choice. Sacrifices had to be made.

He took a step back, aimed the assault rifle at the Master's head and fired.

Only when the rifle's bolt slammed to empty did he ease off the trigger. He threw the weapon on the ground and fell to his knees, crushed by the weight of his decision. The Master was finished and the Enclave was shattered, but he'd sentenced Erica Kearns to death. He sucked in a few short breaths, releasing them in ragged heaves. A hand came down on his shoulder and gripped it.

Charlesworth.

Herron muttered. "It's over. He's dead. So is Frances. I'm sorry."

"I thought she'd died years ago." Charlesworth fought back his tears. "Doesn't seem like it's over for you, though."

Herron nodded. "He's been keeping tabs on a

friend of mine. She'll die now. Her life was the price of ending this."

"Learn from my experience." Charlesworth glanced at Frances' body. "No mission is worth the life of someone you love."

"It doesn't matter." Herron sighed again. "I made the choice already." He only hoped that when the Master's phone rang and he was unable to give the password, that the operative ended Erica's life quickly.

"Where is your friend?"

"In the States." Herron climbed to his feet. "Maryland."

"Britain has assets there." Charlesworth pulled out his cell phone. "Give me a location and we'll keep her safe."

Herron frowned. "Why would you do that? You've lived up to your end of the bargain already. I said I'd submit myself to you once the Master was killed."

"Because I think you're a good man who's trying to redeem himself. You tried to save my men by alerting us to the ambush, you saved my life and you didn't kill my daughter when you had the chance." Charlesworth gave a sad smile. "And because I don't want you to suffer the same loss I have for simply doing your duty."

Herron was stunned by the offer. He checked his watch. "Send assets to the McDonalds in Frederick, Maryland. She'll be there for breakfast in an hour from now."

Charlesworth nodded and made the call. After

speaking for a moment, he asked Herron to describe Kearns and relayed the description, then ended the call. "She'll be safe."

"Thanks. Now I'm yours to do what you want."

Charlesworth held up a hand. "You're free to go. And I suggest you go quickly and far from the Western countries. I can only offer a limited amount of protection."

Herron watched in disbelief as Charlesworth turned and walked out the front door of the house, leaving Herron with the bodies of Frances Charlesworth and the Master.

It felt strange that Herron's enemy was dead without his ever knowing the man's real name, but it also seemed fitting. Like the Enclave, the Master would now fade into obscurity.

Lazarus wouldn't rise after all.

It was over.

MORE FROM STEVE P. VINCENT

stevepvincent.com/books

ACKNOWLEDGMENTS

This book was written during a time of significant upheaval for my wife and I.

I couldn't have written this book without the support of Vanessa, my family and friends.

Thanks to my beta readers on this one - Gerard Burg, Dave Sinclair and Janice Harris.

Thanks to Stuart Bache for the amazing cover and Pete Kempshall for the top notch edit.

ABOUT THE AUTHOR

Steve P. Vincent is the USA Today Bestselling Author of the Jack Emery and Mitch Herron conspiracy thriller series.

Steve has a degree in political science, a thesis on global terrorism, a decade as a policy advisor and training from the FBI and Australian Army in his conspiracy kit bag.

When he's not writing, Steve enjoys whisky, sports and travel.

You can contact Steve at:
stevepvincent.com
steve@stevepvincent.com

Made in the USA
San Bernardino, CA
11 January 2020